Jealous
Woman

Part One:
The Playboy's
Second Wife

Chapter One

At the desk, when they said she was in 819, I knew or pappy or somebody was doing all right by their Jane, because 19 is the de luxe tier at the Washoe-Truckee, one of our best hotels here in Reno, and you don't get space there for buttons. They're bright, big rooms on the southwest corner, facing the Sierras and overlooking the river, and they cost dough. I didn't state my business, or mention insurance in any way when I rang her. No smart agent would. I just said I was Ed Horner of Edgar Gordon Horner, Inc., and that her husband had asked me to talk to her in connection with a certain matter, so she said come up. And waiting for me, at the door of her suite, a cigarette in one hand and the knob in the other, so she could step inside if she didn't like my looks, was the Jane Delavan you read about in the papers.

Maybe you saw her pictures, but she was better-looking than they were, because it wasn't Hollywood cheesecake that she had, but strictly class, like you see on the society pages, and sometimes it's a little camera-shy. She was medium-size, and a little on the slim side, though there was plenty of shape of a nice, refined kind. But she didn't dress to show it. Her clothes cost plenty, you could see that, but they hung on her loose and careless, so your eye went up one fold and down the other. Her face was long, with plenty of sunburn, and her hair dark, but with red in it. Her eyes were hazel brown, but they had something in them that was going to cost me some sleep before I got done with them. I mean they were beat up. Nobody had blacked them, but life had. She looked you straight enough in the eye, but not for long. Pretty soon she'd be looking at nothing at all, in a set, squinty way, and then she'd catch herself and come back to you, but with a little smile that was more to cover up than make like friendly. It was enough, pretty soon, to start me wondering about her, and unfortunately you don't wonder about one part of a woman and let the rest go. When that starts, you wonder up the line and down the line, and across and between.

But I couldn't honestly say I saw all of that

at the time, even if I felt a little of it. What I saw mainly was a pretty girl that remembered my name from my giving it over the house phone, something an insurance man notices, because he's got to fix names himself. I didn't get to my business right away. I took a walk around the room, admired the view, said how lucky she was to get one of these suites. She said yes, it had taken some wangling. I asked if I could smoke, took out my cigarette case, got out a cigarette, felt for matches, didn't find any, put the cigarette back, snapped the case fairly loud. I never carry matches. If you can make the prospect light you, you're one up on him. He's generally glad to do it, but what he doesn't know is: it's a little personal thing, and once he does it he can't take it back. The time for a brush-off is past.

She lit me, and of course I jumped up very snappy and bowed to thank her and had a look at the lighter. "That's an interesting thing, Mrs. Delavan. May I ask where you got it?"

"At the gift shop in the lobby."

"Well—just the same, it's nice."

"I left my good one, that a soldier made out of a shell and that always lights in New York, and so I went down and got this. It cost $7.50 and I don't think it's a bit interesting and it hardly ever works, but if it has an admirer who am I to argue about it?"

"Anyhow, it's some of that A-1 local Reno stuff."

"If that be a point in its favor."

". . . Somebody been gypping you?"

"Those blue chips. A bit expensive, I'd say."

"Oh, *them.*"

"I was warned about the gambling, but—"

"Hey, hey, hey! It's straight! Why, if they so much as thought one of their dealers had turned a crooked card they'd not only fire him, Mrs. Delavan, they'd put him in jail."

"Well, it's simply wonderful to know that instead of loaded dice it was Honesty Boys and their simple, barefoot, galloping percentage that took my money. I'm broke, just the same—or almost. It's going to be two weeks before I can do anything at all. I'm furious at myself."

"Oh, we got plenty to do here—practically free."

"What, for instance?"

"You like to fish?"

"No."

"Shoot?"

"No."

"Ride?"

"Now *there's* a nice cheap sport."

"Not so fast, not so fast. We got a little number here called the Scout. It's a dude ranch, but I keep a horse there and he's yours at any time you ring Jackie and tell her to get him ready."

Well, not quite, if you know what I mean. I keep a horse there, and his name is Count Ten, which will give you some idea of the blood that's in him. But anybody that would let a perfect stranger, and a girl at that, ride a thoroughbred horse, is plain crazy, and maybe I am, but not that crazy. But how would she know? For a pretty girl and a $100,000 sale, I could ring Jackie and have her saddle Bingo, who would put her back with his teeth, if she happened to fall off. "If you do like to ride, there needn't be anything very expensive about it."

"You seem most anxious to please me."

"Why not? Your husband sure pleased me."

"Do you mind giving me a rough idea of your business?"

"Insurance."

Her face went hard. "I'm not interested in insurance, and I don't believe my husband sent you here to talk about it."

"You ought to be interested, and he did send me." I gave it to her, what he had told me, and I was casual, friendly and not too long-drawn-out. But the more I talked the more she burned, and pretty soon there was nothing for me to do but cut. Something was here I didn't understand, and until I knew what it was I couldn't go on. When I shut up she began to talk. "In the first place, everything my husband seems to have said to you is true. He has told you nothing that isn't true, and yet he has not told you the slightest part of his real reason for taking out this insurance."

"Which is?"

"If you don't mind, I'm going to talk to him." She went in the bedroom, and in a minute I heard her voice on the phone. I could hear a little of it, and mainly it seemed to be: "Tom, you simply cannot do this thing to me. I can't face it, and believe me it will have consequences you don't even suspect"—stuff like that. So of course that made it perfectly ducky, because whatever it was that she meant I'd have to report what she said and that's when the trouble would start.

It was quite some time before she came out, and when she did she had on riding clothes. They weren't Western, like girls wear in Nevada, with tight dungarees, stitched boots, and cowboy hats. They were whipcord breeches, high boots, tailored coat, and derby hat, and crop, like they wear to the Eastern horse shows. She stood there a minute, pulling on her gloves and then: "Mr. Delavan will speak to you about the insurance. Apparently I have no voice in the matter, one way or the other, except to protest, so I'd rather not be bothered about it any more, if you don't mind."

"There's just one thing."

"I'd rather you spoke to him."

"I'm trying to tell you: Hara-kiri's out."

"I beg your pardon?"

"We don't pay off on suicide."

"That's not what he's up to."

"I heard some of your call, and it sounded like it."

"Then you don't pay off on suicide."

"I just want you to know. And him to know."

"I rang Jackie, by the way, and she's getting me a horse. Do you mind if I go? It's getting late, and I shouldn't like to get caught in this country with night coming on."

"Do you have a car?"

"I'm taking a cab."

"I'll ride you out."

I rode her out and arranged to bring her back, and took Jackie aside and said if she showed any signs of being able to ride she should have a run on the Count. But where I went then, as fast as I could scoot into town, was the Sierra Manor, to see Delavan, her husband, and find out what it was all about. I preferred talking to him there than at my office, where he had come earlier in the day. I told him what she'd said and told him to put it on the line and put all of it on the line. "Just a minute, Mr. Horner. There's something in your manner I don't wholly like. You act as though I've concealed things from you."

"Well, *she* says you have."

"Pardon me, Mr. Horner, but I'll decide what's relevant."

"No. I will. What's back of this?"

"An action for annulment."

"That's she's bringing?"

"That I am."

"Then what's she doing here?"

"She came here for the usual six-weeks period of residence, expecting to get a divorce. With my knowledge, of course. But my situation changed. I couldn't let her."

"How did it change?"

10

"The lady I expect to marry objected."

"What did she have to do with it?"

"Though American, she's the grand-daughter of an Anglican bishop. These people have strong, almost unshakable convictions on the remarriage of divorced persons. So long as there was no help for it, she was willing to give up the church wedding, performed by her own rector, a thing that means a great deal to her. But when a chance remark of mine, made a couple of weeks ago, just after Jane left for the West, showed that grounds for annulment existed, the whole picture changed and she demanded that I take advantage of my opportunity. I've run into a pretty thick situation with her, I can tell you, and not only with her but the family. If I can get an annulment I have to do it."

". . . Annulment? You mean—you and your wife have been married in name only?"

"No, I mean her first divorce may have been defective. You've heard about corespondent unknown?"

"Yes, of course."

"Except she wasn't unknown."

"Oh, that was bad judgment."

"They let Jane's maid make the $500."

"Is the maid here?"

"I'm serving her papers today."

"As a material witness?"

"Yes. Compelling her to give bond."

"But what does she know?"

"That the alleged infidelity, on the part of Jane's former husband, was a complete phony, cooked up by Jane, the husband, and the maid. That the whole divorce was collusive, based on manufactured evidence."

"Well, no wonder she's sore."

"She has no reason."

"Except she'll still be married to No. 1."

"Don't be silly. He's married again."

"Then he'll be a bigamist."

"Nowhere but in Nevada and on the basis of a Nevada decision."

"But you still feel guilty?"

"It upsets me, yes."

"And you want this insurance so you can begin taking the curse off it? So you can feel like a hero instead of a heel?"

"In case of eventuality, yes."

He began to falter and stammer, and then to talk fast and jerky, but straight to the point, as well as I could see. I mean, he got to it at last, the reason for this $100,000 straight life policy he had come in to see me about this morning. He had very little money, he said, in spite of his name, which he seemed to think had made me drop in a faint when I heard it, on account of the dough his family was supposed to have. It meant nothing to me, which may prove how ignorant I am, or on the other hand how big the country is. Anyhow, in West Virginia was an old coal mine he owned, that had been closed down, but that opened up again when some kind of a machine was invented that made operation profitable where they'd been in the red before. And he'd got a dividend check of two or three thousand dollars that he didn't expect. And what he wanted to do was sock this dough into the first premium of the life policy, so his wife would be protected the first year after the annulment, and he would feel easier in his mind about it. I said: "What about the second year?"

". . . I may have to let it lapse."

"So I judge. But I mean about her?"

"Mr. Horner, do I have to go on with this marriage for the rest of my life? Jane and I made a mistake, but in marriage a mistake takes two to make. Once it's erased from the ledger, why not be honest about it? Jane is a well-bred, good-looking girl, who's going to get married again and make some guy a swell wife. That's fine with me, and I wish her, and him when he comes, everything that life can give them. But I see no need for overlap. All I think is necessary is to see that she's protected in the near future—as I said, in case of eventuality. In the case of an annulment, no alimony, property settlement, or anything of the kind is possible, since of course it is merely the legal declaration that no marriage existed. But if I should die. in the near future, if for some reason I did come into money and a large estate were settled, I don't want her left out completely in the cold. Does that answer all your questions?"

It did, or I thought it did, even if it struck me he was more interested in going through the motions of protecting her than actually doing it. I mean, it seemed to me he was going to kid himself he was actually making her a present of $100,000, and square it up with himself for the way he figured to leave her, neither married or not married, just dangling in mid-air, with no court to take her side, because mixing it up that way is what most of the courts, including our 100% wonderful Supreme Court, seem to be fondest of. But I didn't see, on my end of it, why I was called on to step in and block the insurance in any way, whether she was squawking or not. Because in the first place, it's practically impossible to convince an agent he's doing anybody an injury, or in fact anything but a favor, in helping them become beneficiary of any kind of policy at all. And in the second place, there was kind of a personal reason I'd better be on the level about, as later the subject came up. My company, the General Pan-Pacific of California, General Pan for short, gives an annual cup to the agent making the best score for the year, all averaged up so the fellow in a small city has just as good a chance as a big city general agent, and my first few years, when I was just a kid, I collected four of those, one right after the other. But when Washington upped the high Army brass from four stars to five, the home office upped General Pan, because until then the cup had four stars on it, for his rank. And that new one, with five stars all in a cluster, I hadn't been able to get, and I wanted it, and specially before my thirtieth birthday, so bad I could cry. With this $100,000 policy, I'd grab it in a walk. And it was none of my business if next year he let it lapse or not. Plenty of policies lapse, and the contest had no rule covering that. If I wrote the business, and he paid the first premium due, that was that, and that was all. So when he finished, and I thought it over, and said O.K. I'd shoot his application though, I could feel my heart doing flip-flops inside. General Five-Star Cup, come to baby.

Chapter Two

When I got back to the stable, my friend Mrs. Delavan had the Count on the track, and Jackie was out there watching it. I mean it was something to see. He was under an English saddle, with curb bit and martingales, and my own Western saddle was nowhere around. Believe it or not, she was walking him. It was the first time I knew he *could* walk. He's a gray, with dark mane and tail, and a comical forelock that makes him look a little like Whirly, if you remember him, and he's a clown, but strictly a dancing clown, not a walking clown. And it took me a minute or two to figure it out. There was 105 pounds of will power on his back that said walk and he walked. In a minute her feet shifted and he went into a canter, then into a dead run. It was beautiful, the way he obeyed. I mean, he loved it the way she handled him, and he was letting her know it, every move that he made, how he liked to go when there was somebody up there that knew how to make him go. She pulled him down to a trot, and then, so sudden you wondered why she didn't go over his head, to a walk, and came on over. "What on earth, Mr. Horner, have you been doing with this horse?"

"Riding him. Why?"

"He has no more manners than a baboon."

"He been eating with his knife?"

"I don't think you even know what I'm talking about."

"We get there, he and I, and we get back."

"But it's a crime! What he came into this world with, his looks, his action, are beautiful. But what you've taught him, if anything, is simply embarrassing."

Jackie began sicking her finger at me, because she'd been telling me for some time that now that I had a horse it might be a good idea to learn something about him. I gave her the old so's-your-old-man and we went in the ring, where the jumps are. He went into one of those whirling movie starts I had impressed the girls with. I thought it was pretty nifty, but she pulled him down stockstill before his front feet were halfway up in the air. "This is really dreadful."

"I like it, that stunt."

"There ought to be a horse court that would take him away from you and establish guardianship."

Jackie had told her he'd never been jumped, so she walked him off about fifty feet, turned him, let him look at the jump, then brought him up to it at a slow canter. When he got the idea she raised her hands and leaned forward, and he went over like a cat. She turned him and let him look at it again. He got the comicalest look on his face I ever saw, then she took him over it again. "Put another bar on."

I did and he took it so easy I started to put on another. "Wait a minute. That we'll have to think about." She got down, lit a cigarette, studied him, and he did the same for her. She patted him and he nuzzled her. Then she stamped out the cigarette. "O.K."

I put the bar on and she rode him off and turned him. She let him look at it, then started him for it, and for the first time I felt a prickle of nervousness shoot up my spine. They came on, he hooked it up, she let off the reins and leaned forward, and he went up. It was a frightening thing to be under because all of a sudden you felt it, the power in those muscles, when it was

18

delivered, all in a bunch, right where it was wanted, and when. And you felt it, how high that jump was.

They were over, and down with such a rush you could hardly believe one slim leg could take the whole shock and hold for the others to take over. It did though, and they were in stride again. Just then I saw the puppy, and she did, and he did. She swerved him, but he braided his legs. I was there as soon as she hit the ground, but she had had just enough warning to be able to fall clear. I knelt beside her, and she seemed to like it that my arm was around her. Then she sat up and opened her eyes, and a look of horror came into them. I looked, and the Count was still lying there, with Jackie racing toward him. Jane jumped up, and just then he did. She went over and put her arms around him. "Baby! Did he knock himself out?"

She went over him, inch by inch, feeling his withers and hocks and every part of him, and he did the same by her with the tip of his nose. But he was all right, and pretty soon we started home. About halfway. she said: "In his fifth year, I make him."

"That's right."

"Then he's young enough, thank heaven."

"For what?"

"To learn. I'm here, and I'm going to teach him."

"He's all yours. Stable suit you?"

"Stable's fine."

When we got to the hotel, a girl in maid's uniform came running across the lobby from where she had been sitting, keeping company with the elevator girl, and waving a paper with a blue cover on it. She was one of those girls you don't hear about in England, but when you go there you see them all over. She was red-haired and black-eyed, and pretty, and had a Cockney way of talking and kept going on about the "bloody garnishee," as she called it. I pretty well knew from my talk with Delavan what it was, and that it wasn't a garnishee, but I kept to myself what I knew.

Jane stood there, reading the paper, and her face got the beat-up look I've mentioned before, and pretty soon she looked up and held out her hand. "I think—I'll go upstairs, if you don't mind."

"I'll ring you."

"Please do."

She and the maid went on up and I went over to my office. I tried to have fun thinking about my cup that was coming. It didn't give me much. I could see Linda, my secretary, looking at me out of the corner of her eye. I told her I was going over to Carson to close a deal, and wouldn't be back. Where I did go was out and walk around.

That night I was still restless, and stepped out a little to get my mind off her and the rest of it. I generally play roulette, but never when I'm feeling good. When I don't give a hoot I fool around with a stack of quarters. If I lose my stack, I go home. If I get ahead, so I'm gambling on their money, I make scientific mayhem out of it, and feel better. Before I saw her, I had shifted tables, and even joints, three or four times. At roulette, if you're winning, you pick up a mob that follows your lead, and right there is where I don't exactly trust Mr. Croupier. He may be honest, as they say he is, and as I firmly believe and tell everybody he is, and yet, I feel you ought not to put irresistible temptation in his way. If the bets are scattered, he has no reason to roll his ball any particular way. But if they're all aboard one number, or a small flock of numbers, every square on the board except those numbers is a winner for the house, and it would be unfortunate if that was the particular moment in his life he picked out to have a slight change of character. Just to be safe, I move. I even move up the street, to really shake them, and I'd done that a few times before I saw her. She seemed sulky and I thought she meant me. I went over to the bar, ordered a couple of the free drinks, and went over and handed her one.

"Thanks, Mr. Horner, but don't let me keep you."

"From what, like?"

"Well, you seem to be avoiding me."

I explained about the powder I'd been taking, and she seemed set back on her heels. "I—never even thought about that. You see, I've never had a winning streak."

"Never too late to learn."

"I've lost too much."

"Let me stake you."

I fished up a couple of pounds of what I'd been winning and chinked them around a little. In Reno, of course, they always pay you silver. "I shouldn't, you know, Mr. Horner. It's a weakness of mine. If you keep rattling all that money around, I'm going to say yes, but—it'll all be gone, I assure you."

"I'll take a chance."

She started to play, and it was the craziest playing I ever saw. She just shut her eyes and plunked it down anywhere. "Hey, hey, that's no way to do it!"

"What's the difference? It's all luck."

"Yeah, but it's got to make sense!"

An insurance man, he thinks percentage, first, last and all the time, because what he's running is not charity for the widows, orphans, and aunts, like maybe you thought, but a great big wheel, with every chance figured by the actuaries, so that a bet is distinctly a matter of age, weight and occupation, and he hates to have anything running wild. So I took the young lady in hand and showed her a few things, like how to cut corners on a losing streak by running a small limit and fishing for small fish, like the 2-1 odds on one of the 12s, which some chance of two or three wins that would cause the switch from a losing streak to a winning streak. Once that happened, I showed her how to bunch her bets so as not to be on the hook for too much dough on any single roll, but at the same time to crack a pot if she really got a break. I showed her how, if she had $1 riding the first twelve, she should lay 50¢ on the first four and 25¢ on No. 1. Then, if the pill fell away from No. 13 up, she had lost, but was only $1.75 out, and as she would be playing on their money, she could afford it. But if the ball fell in any number of the first 12, she cashed $2, and was 25¢ ahead. But if it fell in 2, 3 or 4, she cashed $2 on the first 12 and $4.50 on the first 4, and was $6.50 ahead. But if the ball rolled in 1, she not only cashed her $2 and $4.50, but $9, the pay-off on 25¢ at the odds of 36-1, and really did something for herself. "In other words, if you've got Lady Luck sitting there beside you, act like you knew how to treat her so she don't have to be a contortionist to help you out. Besides, the way you do it, how would you know her? She doesn't like it when you don't place her face, any more than anybody else does."

So she got hot, and I gave her her head. She caught a gang pretty soon, and we moved. She upped her bets and I said O.K. I picked up her money, and got so heavy with silver I felt like a pack donkey, but when she dropped three $5 combos I walked off and out. "But please. Give me some money! I'm winning! I—"

"Then quit!"

"You're hateful! Now, to deny me—"

"I'm the best friend you've got."

On the street, when I put handful after handful of money in her handbag, so it felt like a suitcase full of bricks, she laughed.

"It's the one silly streak I've got. On a horse, I'm a woman of ice. At other things I'm not stupid, I assure you. But when I get into one of these places I go crazy."

"That $227 will calm you down."

"Is that what I won?"

"About."

"Want to walk?"

On the bridge near her hotel we stopped and watched the water rushing along under the moon, and when I looked I saw somebody I hadn't known was there. I mean, up to now, allowing for stuff you might see in any woman that was jangled up over what her husband was pulling, she had been just what Delavan had said, a well-born dame that might meet somebody before long, but didn't live where I lived. Now, though, she was just a nice girl, nothing snooty, nothing horsey, just a girl with a guy on a bridge.

"Do you realize, Mr. Horner, that you did something peculiar today?"

"And specially tonight, when I let you do the winning."

"Today you came to me, not to your beautiful horse."

"I should have, shouldn't I?"

"Just doing your duty?"

"Why, sure."

"Anyway, thanks."

She looked away quick, and I felt like a heel, because she didn't mean anything but a little flirting under the moon, but just to be sociable I could have played up to it. I wanted to, don't get me wrong about that. Just the same, I've got a policy on that stuff. Until that application was signed, sealed, and forwarded with report of medical examination to the home office, no romance on the bridge for Ed Horner. I took her home and said good night. Couple of nights later I bumped into her again and helped her win some more. Moving from one place to another, she'd put her hand on my arm and I'd catch her looking at me, like maybe I was dumb on horses, but I had a few other things she liked. In the meantime, I had Delavan examined by the doctor, got his check, and sent his papers through to Los Angeles. Then I felt free to call her. "How do you feel about dinner tonight, Mrs. Delavan?"

"Well, let me see, how do I feel?"

"Just inquiring."

"My maid is summoned to court. Oh, that's right, you were there when she told me about it. Her case comes up at four and I'll have to be there, as it's a question of bail."

"That oughtn't to take all day."

"Then I'll be free."

"Around seven?"

"I'll expect you."

I went to the hearing, just to keep the record straight, and sat in the back of the room. Delavan was there, and the maid, and Jane, and a couple of lawyers. It took about ten minutes. The maid was held, in $250 bail, and Jane took cash out of her handbag and put it up. I felt kind of proud I had a little something to do with that cash. She wasn't broke any more.

That night I expected her to be upset, but she didn't show any ill effects, and we went to the Bonanza for dinner. Then I drove her to Virginia City, the old mining town, for a brandy at a bar there, and after that we took a walk on the boardwalk to look at the pioneer stuff. Then we came back to Reno for a little more circular golf, and she won a little, but not much. Then we strolled over to my office to look up the Count's pedigree, so she could see where those gaits came from. When I put on the desk lights she spotted the cups and brought one over to read the engraving on it. Then she said: "You're such a funny thing."

"How?"

"Such a—go-getter."

"Is that funny?"

"But I mean it as a compliment!"

"Then O.K."

"My world is oh, so veddy well-bred. In plain English, well-heeled. Well-heeled heels that would regard go-getting as a distinct social solecism."

"As—*what?*"

"I just said that to see your face. As a distinct breach of form. But you, you really like to bring home that cup, don't you?"

"And I do it, don't make any mistake about that."

"I like you for it." She took my head in her hands and put a little soft kiss on my mouth. I put my arm around her and pulled her to me, to mean it. "No, please."

"If not, why not?"

"I'm still married. It would be messy."

On the doorknob, when we came in, had been a notice of a wire. So when she began looking up the pedigree I rang to find out what it was. They read it to me, and it was from Los Angeles, and I saved it:

DELAVAN POLICY MAILED YOU TODAY
BUT HOLD DELIVERY PENDING FURTHER

ORDERS. MR. KEYES ARRIVING YELLAND
FIELD TEN TOMORROW WEDNESDAY A.M.
REGARDS

NORTON

When I finally got her home, and said good
night at the elevators, and went around to
the Fremont, where I lived, and got to my
apartment, I hit the roof. I cussed, I raved,
I stomped around, till the desk rang up to
know if there was something wrong. Then
I tried liquor and that didn't work. Finally
I went to bed, but don't get the idea I went
to sleep. Norton is president of the company
and Keyes is head of the claim department,
a bird we got not long ago from another of
the Norton group of companies, and there
was no claim on the Delavan policy yet but
he gets called in on all kinds of stuff that the
underwriters don't know what to do about,
and without hearing any more about it this
meant trouble. With Keyes in it it would be
just plain agony, because if there was any
twisted, cock-eyed, queer angle that could
be found on it, he'd turn it up, and about
two dozen of his own that nobody else could
find in it, but that he had to see just to show
what a genius he was at it.

Chapter Three

I hadn't seen him since two or three cases he'd had that had got a lot of space in the newspapers, and while I had heard about the way he was playing up to it, and the reporters at the airport should have tipped me off, I wasn't quite ready for what came off the plane. In the first place, he had lost about fifty pounds, because while he wasn't exactly a slim, slanky cowboy type even now, he was rightdown beautiful compared with the Berkshire hog type he had been before. In the second place, the clothes he wore, from the down-on-one-side hat to the tailormade suit, were just like what a picture actor wears on a personal appearance tour. And in the third place, he had that look in his eye that says camera. He saw me and waved, and then looked surprised as anything at the reporters at the gate, though how they would be there if somebody hadn't tipped them off, I couldn't quite figure out. He stood twenty minutes being interviewed, on the political situation, the business outlook, and the crime wave, which all hands seemed to know about, though it was the first I'd heard there was one. Then I drove him to the Washoe-Truckee, where I had tried to get him a de luxe suite, but there weren't any, so they gave him a nice single on the east side of the hotel and we walked over to my office. I sat him behind my desk, put the Delavan folder in front of him, went out to see some prospects, and told Linda I'd ring in from time to time to see if he was ready to talk. So when I got back around five it turned out his idea of when to talk was that night after dinner. I had to call Mrs. Delavan and break my date. "I'm sorry, but there's a shot here from the home office and there's nothing much I can do."

"Well, Mr. Horner, does it really matter?"

"It does to me."

"Then maybe you've forgotten something."

"Which is?"

"The gambling houses never close—why not—why not, *Ed?*"

"Say, say, say."

"Put him bidey-bye and ring Jingle-Janey."

After dinner I took him to a picture, and around eleven there didn't seem to be any place he could go but bed. So I took him to my hotel. I waved as he went up in the car, and he was hardly out of sight when I dived for the house phone.

"But, Ed, who's the shot?"
    "Just head of the claim department."
    "Anything wrong?"
    "No. Why?"
    "You seem greatly preoccupied."
    "Preoccupied with color."
She had on slacks and a mink coat, with red bag, red shoes, and a red ribbon around her hair, and the way I told it, it had given me the idea for a whole new system based on betting the red. It cost me $18 before we switched to something that made sense, but she thought it was hot stuff and forgot about everything else. But then, as we took a drift over to some new place to change our luck, my heart stood still because there at a chuck-a-luck game stood Keyes. I pulled her back on the street. "But what—?"
    "The shot from the home office."
    "Well?"
    "Jane, I'd rather he didn't see me."
    "Doing exactly what he's doing?"
    "He's on a trip, and if he makes it a toot, well—they all do. But me, I'm home, and if it looks like I did it every night, that's different."

We started down the street, her hand on my arm, as it generally was now, but her head was down, like she was thinking. And pretty soon she said: "I have the queerest feeling."

"About the red? It's not good."

"About the shot from the home office. I keep thinking it's not the roulette you don't want him to see, but me."

"That's ridiculous."

"It would certainly seem so, and yet—"

After awhile she stopped and faced me. "Now I've got it. . . . The insurance deal is still on, isn't it?"

"Listen, I bring home cups."

"And this man's investigating, isn't he?"

"He might be."

"Will you send him to me?"

"What for?"

"I might block this insurance."

"This is not a guy I can send places, to you or anybody. This is Mr. Keyes, that regards himself as a national celebrity, and maybe he takes my advice, and maybe he doesn't. And anyway, I've got enough trouble with him already without fixing it up for you to make me a little more."

"To you this is just insurance, isn't it?"

"That's all."

"And human questions, they don't matter?"

"Yeah, Jane, but what's insurance got to do with it?"

"Everything."

"That's no answer. Give."

"I can't."

"Why not?"

"I'd involve other people."

"Like who?"

"I can't discuss it with you."

"Then the deal's on."

We went on a little way, then she stopped and right under the bright lights on Virginia Street she took my two coat lapels in her hands. "Ed, can't you take what I say on faith?"

"Afraid not."

"Would I be one to imagine things?"

"I wouldn't say so."

"Then why won't you believe me?"

"You really want to know?"

"You know I do."

"The No. 5 cup."

I told her about the five-star cluster, and all the rest of it. Her eyes got wet, so they glittered. "But that's so childish."

"So's everything."

"But terrible things are at stake."

"What are they?"

"If this wasn't so serious it would be funny."

She put her arms around me, there in front of the hotel, and kissed me, warm and full, the first time she ever had. "You like me a lot, Ed, or so you said."

"I think I'm in love with you."

"I think you are too."

"Jane, are *you* in love with *me?*"

"I'm suffering from a badly bruised heart, and you can't forget everything and be in love at the drop of a hat. But I'm happy when I'm with you, so I guess it's not far off. Now, because you love me, will you drop this whole thing simply because I ask it and tell Tom he can't have his insurance? There's a reason for that. When he finds he can't get insurance he'll be so frightened he'll drop this whole thing he intends to do to me. You see, Tom's whole trouble is he can never take anything seriously. Whether it's marriage, polo, or work, such little work as he does, it's always the same. He makes a game of it. He even has to make a game out of ending his marriage. But if he's a child about such things, he's also a child in his unusual capacity to feel fear. This will scare him to death, and end the whole farce. Promise me, and then we'll go up to

35

my nice little suite and make coffee and you can work on the $64 question: What have you got that makes me want to run my fingers through your hair?"

I didn't promise, but I kissed her, and I can kid myself all I please, but I know now, and I knew then, that she took it as a promise. Well, why did I go up with her, have coffee, spend one of those romantic hours, and not bring the thing up any more, to make it all clear, how I stood? I think I've told you, an agent thinks he's doing anybody a swell turn to get a policy written for them, whether it's for one year or twenty. And by that time, I had come to the conclusion that whatever it was she meant by all the fuss she was kicking up, it didn't amount to much, or wouldn't, once she combed Delavan out of her hair. On top of that, I'll admit it, I wanted the cup, but I could see no reason, no reason that made any sense at all, why I couldn't have the cup and her too, or at least have a wonderful time with her, and the works later, with orange blossoms, if that's how it turned out. Then O.K., O.K., I'll say it again:

I wanted that cup.

And, believe it or not, I told Keyes what had

been said, when he came to the office next morning after talking with Delavan. So far, I had told him nothing about her. But the way I did it, like leaving out her asking me to promise, was proof that down deep in me I wasn't really telling all I knew, I was just going through the motions. I kept saying to myself it was "personal," whatever that meant, and nobody's business but my own. He hardly heard me. "I don't see anything to this but a playboy that's come into an unexpected piece of change and has figured a way to pretend to himself he's going to do something pretty nice for her to square up for giving her a dirty deal on the annulment."

"That's how I see it."

"And there might be a blow-hard angle."

"In what way, Mr. Keyes?"

"In his clubs, or wherever he hangs out. It's around, don't worry, how little she's getting, because he even admits it isn't enough. But if he can toss it off about the 'six-figure insurance deal' that was put on top of it, that'll get around too. Once it's around, what does he care? He's taken care of his name, and at the end of a year he can quit worrying. As he says, she'll probably be married anyway. He's probably patting himself on the back, what a noble guy he is. And there may be a tax angle we don't know about."

"You don't seem to believe much in nobility."

"In a word, no."

"What do you make of her, Mr. Keyes?"

"Well, who *would* want this annulment?"

"Yeah, but what's blocking the insurance got to do with it?"

"It's not so dumb, once you meet the guy. She probably figures that if you take away his chance to look noble, the rest of it'll be so raw that even he won't have the gall to go through with it. Ed, he's a silly guy. She knows him. She's got her reasons. Of course, if there was somebody around that would plug him for what he's doing, that would be different. Fortunately, we can eliminate that."

"Oh, can we?"

"Well, you wouldn't, would you?"

"What have I got to do with it?"

"Well, you're going around with her."

"On business, a little."

"Like a little necking in front of the hotel?"

"Says who?"

"I saw you . . . She was such a pretty girl

I stopped at the desk and asked who she was. I think it can be assumed if she's having hot smackeroos with you, she's not having them with somebody else. He won't get shot, in my humble opinion."

"This all came after his application was in."

"It's O.K. with me."

"I'm kind of stuck on her."

"I don't fall for them as a rule. I've got a superstition about it. Somehow, I feel that's all it would need, for me to fall for one, and here it would come, all ready-made from up yonder, a chapter at a time. Stories are wonderful things—but from the outside looking in, Ed, every time. From the inside looking out, not so good."

It crossed my mind, driving out to see one of the Count's lessons in manners, could I be on the inside of something, looking out, and not know it?

Keyes had got the company to make it a rule that anything in six figures gets a special check, whether there's anything questionable or not, so that meant he had to sit around till he got his report from New York. That meant I'd have to entertain him, but there was no help for it, so I rang her and said I'd meet her later. Around five o'clock he rang me at the office, and from the way he stuttered I began to wonder what *he* wanted. "Listen, Mr. Keyes, is there something else *you'd* rather do?"

"Oh, not at all, but—"

"Spill it."

"There's somebody I'd like to invite."

"Hey, hey, hey. And ho, ho, ho. And ha, ha, ha."

"Oh, it's nothing like that. She's married and rich and wants nothing from me. Just the same, she's a pretty good looker, and I thought—"

"Who is she?"

"Nobody you know. She's from Bermuda."

"If she's getting it melted, watch out."

"No. She's here on business—cashing chips."

"She won't be rich long."

"She can afford it."

"She's all yours."

"Couldn't we invite—your little friend, Ed?"

"I don't think she'd go for it."

"Ed, can I say something?"

"Shoot!"

"Personal?"

"O.K."

"Watch out."

"Well, the same to you and many of them."

"Don't worry about me, my young friend. But you, you could be starting something you can't stop."

That night I took Jane over to Carson, and she loved it, because it's the tiniest state capital in the world, and she said it was like tip-toeing around in some doll's house. After we had dinner at the Arlington we started up the Bridgeport Road, because over the California line, in the high country where there's real forest, you often see deer and other big game, and she thought she would like that. She was feeling good, and before long I found out why. "I think my difficulty's near an end. I think my problem is going to be solved, and soon. I think it'll all get straightened out before I, or Tom, complete our six weeks' period of residence."

"Gee, that's swell."

"In town has arrived a lady."

"You interest me strangely."

"The present wife of my former husband."

"To get Tom to lay off the annulment?"

"I can imagine no other reason."

"Who is your former husband, by the way?"

"Richard Sperry."

"I never heard of him."

"He was well enough known when I married him. His scientific standing as a petroleum expert is good and solid. Backed up by her money, though, he's become internationally eminent. And I imagine her money will tell the story here."

"You mean—she'll offer Tom?"

"I think so."

"And Tom will take it?"

She talked along about society people, and what they will do for money, or even free booze, like endorse this, that, or the other brand of whiskey, and I got the idea friend Tom could be had, and maybe cheap. We saw a deer and a pair of eyes we decided was a puma, though if you ask me, most of those pumas along the road would yip like coyotes if you coaxed them with a rock. She took my hand and patted it. "Yes, I think we can assume that little Connie didn't come all the way from Bermuda, as much money as *she* has, just to say please."

". . . Your husband live in Bermuda?"

"Didn't I say? He's a geologist for the oil companies."

"Didn't know Bermuda had any oil."

"Bermuda's his base. You *can't* live in Venezuela. It's too hot, and they've got malaria."

"How'd she find out about this annulment?"

"Through the frizzle-haired simpleton."

"His fiancee?"

"Who's reached the bragging stage now."

"Would her bragging reach Bermuda?"

"It's practically a suburb of New York."

"She certainly got here quick."

"What's the matter, Ed?"

"Nothing."

"Have I upset you, talking about Dick?"

"Not at all."

"Well, something's eating on you."

"I said nothing's the matter."

We drove to the hotel, but Bermuda, the policy, and the pass at Keyes certainly seemed more than coincidence.

Chapter Four

They say a zebra, as long as he can see the lion, goes on grazing without getting too much excited about it. But when he can't see him, and can only hear him, and has no idea where the sound is coming from, he gets so nervous he can't eat, can't run, and can't stand still. I was that way about Keyes. When he didn't come in next day and he didn't call, I stood it until noon, but by that time I had to find out what he was doing. I drove over to the hotel, and he was in the barber shop. The barber was working on his head, the shine boy on his feet, and the manicure girl on his paws. When I went bug-eyed he acted like nothing had happened, though you could tell from the way Marguerite had to cue him that he'd never had a manicure in his life, and I wouldn't bet much he'd ever had a shine.

In the lobby, when the production job was done, so he shone and squeaked and smelled, he propositioned me about my car. "As there's absolutely nothing I can do until I hear from New York, I'd kind of like to drive Mrs. Sperry around, and if you could accommodate me—"

"It's yours. Here's the key."

"But if you need it I can rent one."

"You? In a U-Drive jalopy?"

"Oh, I drive."

"But you're so valuable to the company."

"I guess that's right."

He was pretty solemn about it, and I deadpanned, though I kind of liked the gag, and I filed it away so in case I had to make a speech at a company banquet I'd have something to tell the boys. Pretty soon he said: "She knows the country and is going to show me a lot of things, like the old mines in Goldfield and Tonopah and Virginia City—those are ghost towns, aren't they?"

"They were, till fires burned the ghostly garments up."

"Extraordinary woman, Ed. Wonderful mind. I was telling her about this problem of ours."

"Yeah? I'm a little surprised."

"Oh, I mentioned no names."

"Then of course that makes it different."

"She thinks as I do, that on big things, you instinctively know what you think, with no evidential substantiation. Beautiful phrase, Ed."

"Here we call it playing a hunch."

"Her mind constantly parallels mine."

"Or yesses it."

". . . What did you say?"

"I said what does she think of our problem?"

"Just what we think. She was wondering if she had any capacity for this clairvoyance of mine, as she calls it, and I laid it out for her. She said, 'Well, it would be terribly exciting if I could feel something steal up and touch me on the shoulder, but I don't. All I see is a somewhat pathetic boy trying to make himself look big in a cheap, silly way.'"

"That makes three of us."

"Got to run, Ed. Mrs. Sperry is waiting."

"To say nothing of the former Mrs. Sperry."

"Who?"

"Jane, waiting for me."

"Mrs. Delavan was the former Mrs. Sperry?"

"Now you got it."

He sat there a long time, sometimes asking me questions about who these people were, and I could see his mind racing up one part of it and down the other, putting everything together, checking what he had said to La Sperry, what she had said to him, and so on. Then he said: "It's none of my business what she's here for, is it, Ed?"

"That I couldn't say."

"And none of hers, what I'm here for."

"That I couldn't say either."

"You know how I dope it out?"

"No, but I'd like to."

"She had no idea what I was telling her."

"What do you mean, telling her."

"About Delavan's policy."

"Had no idea who you were talking about?"

"I never reject a *simple* explanation, Ed."

"That explanation, I'd say, verges on the simple-minded. If you think, after what you told her, she had no idea who you were talking about—that is, if you told her all about the coal company, the—"

"Ouch, I forgot that."

"It's not possible she didn't guess. . . . Mr. Keyes, if you told her about it, as you say, it wasn't up to her to tip it she knew who you were talking about if she didn't want to. Maybe she's a well-mannered dame that doesn't tip things because she was brought up not to. But that's not all. You didn't only tell her. She pumped it out of you. She—"

"No, no, Ed. Nobody could. Not out of me."

"O.K. You're a clam.

He sat another ten minutes thinking. "But what *interest* could she have? What could it mean to her whether Delavan gets his insurance or didn't? She hasn't tried to influence me in any way."

"She's here to block that annulment."

"O.K., now we're getting somewhere."

"Just where?"

"If she's here to block the annulment, by whatever suasion she cares to use—"

"On checks."

"You mean she'll *bribe* Delavan?"

"Why, Mr. Keyes, such language!"

"It's what you mean, isn't it?"

"You think he's too refined to accept?"

I took him out to where the car was parked, and he stood beside it, thinking some more. "I think we've got it, Ed. Mrs. Delavan got that thing they use all over the British Empire, one of those cut-and-dried, found-him-with-an-unknown-woman, in-and-out-in-ten-minutes divorces, and they're perfectly good—so long as everybody plays ball. But God help you if somebody kicks the beans in the fire. An English court will reopen the case sure as God made little apples, and remember, if they wanted to call it on them, this would involve perjury, contempt of court, manufacture of evidence, collusion, everything that mocks the dignity of the court, and that it can't have publicly proved. Delavan thinks he'll kick over the beans. Mrs. Sperry has other ideas, because she doesn't propose to have her marriage ruined by a playboy's caprice. So far as I'm concerned, that accounts for everything, her trip here, all of it."

I made sure he knew where the starter was and went off and left him. Why I had talked so tough I don't know, as the hand as it was dealt said I ought to have talked the other way. But somehow, even if it is against your own interest, you can blow your top a little when you see a guy kidding himself and shutting his eyes to what he ought to be seeing. Because, tough talk or not, ramming the probe in, pretending to go into it from the company angle or however I played it, there was stuff going on here I didn't understand, and my stomach was telling me it was no good.

Going into the week-end it was high, wide and handsome, with Jane and me out with the horses most of the time, and he running the roads with Mrs. Sperry. But when he brought her in Saturday morning, to pick up tickets for the football game over at the University, I didn't exactly like her, but I could see what he'd fallen for. She was a little older than Jane, maybe a little under thirty, small and stocky, but not fat. But in the blue dress with white spots on it that she was wearing, with tan shoes, hat and bag and fur coat, you could hardly miss that trim, pretty shape, with nice legs that reminded you somehow of a cat. Or maybe it was her eyes that did that. Her face was round, with puffy, dimpled cheeks, rosebud mouth and small, perky nose and light hair; but her eyes were the diamond shape you see in a leopard, and light gray.

But she didn't look like anybody else, you had to say that for her, and when she smiled at me and clucked over the cups and made herself friendly with Linda, you couldn't exactly kick her in the teeth. She made my skin prickle a little, and yet I'm human and it wasn't just to be nice to Keyes that I put myself out for her. After some talk about the football game she said: "I hear you see little Jane Delavan."

"Yes, we ride a little."

"Lovely girl."

". . . You know her?"

"Well—that would be a little complicated. But I've seen her and heard a lot about her—and I know a lot of people that she knows."

"Shall I remember you to her?"

"I think it would please her that I spoke pleasantly of her. But if you mention it, don't say anything as coming from me."

"O.K."

But how I was going to do it at all was

what worried me, because to mention it would mean I would have had to mention what Keyes had to do with it, and what was he doing here all this time? But I could have saved myself the trouble of thinking about it, because by dinner Jane already had it. "Ed, I ask you once more what that man is doing here."

"He has business."

"And what's he doing with her?"

"Maybe he likes her."

"What's she doing with him?"

"Vice versa, maybe."

"With her, that's not enough."

"Then maybe she wants a good time."

"Ed, have you kept your promise to me?"

I said I never broke my promises, which sounded a little better than it was.

I'm a member of Unity, and next morning, when service was over at the Masonic Temple, I stepped over to the hotel to see how she felt on the subject of lunch. But Keyes was in the lobby, slumped down in his chair, and when he saw me he jumped up and came over almost at a trot. "Ed, I've got to talk to you. I've been trying to reach you all morning, and—I've got to talk."

"O.K.—talk."

"Not here. I'm not myself."

We went up to his room and first he sat on the bed, then he lay on it. Then he got an envelope out of his pocket, opened it, took out a paper and said: "Read that."

It was one of our operative's reports, and from the first page, where "subject" went to a football game, it was easy to see that who was under surveillance was Mrs. Sperry. "So you got pretty stuck on her, but not so stuck you didn't have her shadowed."

"No, Ed, that's not how it was at all."

"Looks like it."

"The whole thing was routine. I put the case in charge of our Department of Investigation, down in Los Angeles. I told them to take the whole thing over. How did I know they'd decide to include her in their check-up? I'd never even heard of her when I left to come up here. But—and the worst of it is the operative doesn't even know who I am."

I read it, and right near the end it went something like this:

11:05 P.M. Subject returned to hotel, entered suite 642 with Robert Keyes.

11:08 P.M. Keyes left subject's suite.

11:14 P.M. Phone rang in subject's suite, subject answered, conversation inaudible.

11:15 P.M. Subject admitted man to her room. Identity undiscovered so far. Description:

Age: 30-35.
Height: About six feet.
Weight: Around 160.
Hair: Black, slightly gray.
Good build, well-dressed.
At 12:00 P.M. this man had not come out. I put wedges cut from three paper matches in crack between door and frame, using point of penknife to work them into place in such way they would fall unnoticed if door was opened. Went off duty.
Sunday:
9:30 A.M. Wedges still in place.

"Well, Mr. Keyes, she crossed you."
"But why?"
"Maybe she likes him."
"I thought she liked me. I—worshiped her."
"Being married to one guy, playing around with another, carrying on with still another—it's done every day, except mostly

they don't have a private eye down the hall wearing a porter's blouse."

"And I thought she was a lady—a thoroughbred."

"Oh, ladies play, but they don't get caught."

"It's a horrible shock to me."

"Don't say you weren't warned."

"Warned? By whom? Who *dared* warn me?"

"Me. Remember my saying—watch out?"

"That was a gag."

"Or so you thought."

"All right, Ed, you warned me."

When I went to Jane's suite, she was in a worse state, if that was possible, than Keyes was. "Ed, something horrible has happened."

"O.K., let's have it."

"Dick's in town."

"Sperry?"

"He's here to kill Tom."

". . . You mean bump him off? Like that?"

"Just like that."

"Nice guy."

"Oh, yes. Once he tried to kill me."

"Kind of a Bluebeard type, I'd say."

"Don't talk like that. . . . Dick has spent

too many years of his life in places where human life is very cheap, and where assassination is one of the regular ways to accomplish an end, and the cheapest. I—I tell you, we went swimming, and suddenly I knew I was not coming back."

"How?"

"I don't know."

"Well—!"

"Oh, later on it was proved. He knew I knew."

"So?"

"I screamed."

"Loud?"

"I said my foot had touched something."

"And?"

"I said it was rough, like sandpaper."

"Oh, like a shark maybe."

"And that was something even Mr. Sperry couldn't face. He tried to pooh-pooh it, but I screamed again, and he cut for shore."

"Well, there's no ocean here, or sharks."

"Ed, please listen to me. I've tried to tell Tom if he persisted in this thing, this annulment, that Dick would have to do something about it. I told him what I've just told you. I told him Dick was like that, that rather than have this thing happen he would kill him. His answer was to go to you about insurance. To prove he thought it simply silly he looked up an agent in the phone book and went over to your office. Well, thank heaven I warned you in time, and that part is out. That silly gesture he made, to prove I was just dreaming things up, and that even seemed silly to him, when I told him his application would be disapproved. You're protected, but he's not. We've got to think of some way to block this off."

"And with him gone I could marry you."

I guess it was a gag, but before she could answer the phone rang in the bedroom. She dived in there, and when she came back her eyes were shining. "Thank the all-merciful God! That was Tom. He's given up the annulment action."

"Well, that just about fixes everything."

"I hadn't counted on Dick going to see him."

"Turned on the heat, hey?"

"At last Tom knew what I had been trying to tell him. Oh, I know how Dick looked when he came for that little chat. You wouldn't think those quiet, scientific eyes could get that killer look in them, but they can, all right."

"Then let's celebrate."

"Oh, yes!"

"Little trip to Tahoe?"

"I'd love it."

So we had the hotel fix us some lunch and drove up to Tahoe and ate it in the woods, sitting on a rock beside the lake. But before we went I called on Keyes in his room. "News, chum."

". . . What is it, Ed?"

"That guy, last night, was her husband."

He had flopped back on the bed as soon as he let me in, but now he jumped up and grabbed the phone. When the operator told him that yes, Mr. Richard Sperry was registered, I thought his grin would come together at the back of his neck and take off the top of his head. "Ed, you can't know what you've done for me."

"Oh, ye of little faith."

"That thoroughbred, and I suspected her!"

"And the annulment suit's out."

"I bet you're pleased."

"Somewhat."

"Pretty day, isn't it, Ed?"

"That old Nevada air."

Part Two: Dishonorable Intentions

Chapter Five

Of course it didn't quite run straight down Hotsy Totsy Drive, not with Keyes around it couldn't. Next day, when the New York wire cleared everything he called Delavan from my office to tell him it was O.K. Then he began to stall, and then he hung up. And then, after studying the wire some more, he said: "Ed, I think I'm disapproving this risk."

"And why, if I may ask?"

"Concealment."

"Of what?"

"I don't know. But he was surprised."

"At you okaying something?"

"I told him I'd heard from New York, that his application was approved, and he was surprised. He thought it wouldn't be, and there's nothing he's told me or I've told him that should make him think it wouldn't be. That means there's something he expected me to find out. I've got to know what that is."

Now I know why he was surprised. After Jane had told him his application would be disapproved, to be told five days later that it had been passed was enough to surprise anybody. But what I had told her and what she had told him I regarded as completely outside the scope of a company investigation, and if Delavan still wanted to accept his insurance I didn't mean to be blocked off from my cup on some crazy hunch by a guy trying to find stuff that would make headlines in the newspapers. I just calmly got up and walked into the outer office and told Linda to get Mr. Norton on the telephone. Norton's president of the company. He's not quite the man his father was, that founded our company and a couple of other companies and built them up and formulated most of the policies we've got, but he's a nice guy just the same and what I wasn't forgetting in any way, he was a little fed up with Keyes. I spoke to Linda good and loud, so Keyes heard me. When I came back we just sat there, he smoking his cigar and thinking. I smoking mine and burning.

"Mr. Norton?"
"Hello, Horner, what's on your mind?"
I gave him enough of it, even if it was a

long distance call, for him to get what it was about. "Now, Mr. Norton, I've got some cups on my bookcase that say I'm one of the best agents you've got. I've got my eye on another, maybe you know about that. But here's something that maybe you don't know. I've got three letters in front of me, three letters as yet unanswered, from other companies, offering me territory, with general agent rank, in cities a lot bigger than Reno, cities that—"

"Now, Horner!"

"Could mean, to me—"

"Will you let me talk? If you'll meet that afternoon plane, I'll have somebody aboard that I think can straighten things out. Now just take it easy. Play some golf. And let me talk to Keyes."

Keyes hated it, but he had to stand there and say "Yes, sir" every ten seconds, and when he hung up his face was so red it looked like a Technicolor gag. Then he put on his coat and went out.

I expected H. P. Davis, senior vice-president, or maybe Vic Rose, chief of underwriters, but I almost fell over backwards when Norton himself came down the ladder. Oh yes, he did. An insurance company puts first things first, and it knows what the first things are. What brings in its business is agents, and when one of them blows his top even the President's not too proud to jump on a plane. He was just like any other guy as I drove him in, and we went direct to my office, as he was taking the sleeper back and wouldn't need a room at the hotel. "What do they call you, Horner—Ed?"

"My friends do, yes."

"And my name is Jason—Jace if you like me."

"I'd feel funny about that."

"Oh, this is the West."

"Yeah, but a corporation president, he ought not to have people getting familiar. J. P., though, I'd like that all right."

Well, that made him laugh, so by the time we hit town we were getting along fine. Keyes was there when we came in, looking pretty thick, but we went all over it, and then Norton took charge: "Keyes, you knew my father pretty well?"

"Better than you did, perhaps."

"On insurance, I'm sure you did. But I knew him too, and on questions like this, I've heard him say a thousand times: 'Insurance is the assumption of risk. Pig-iron under water is a perfect risk, but nobody takes out a policy on it. That's what the underwriter must always bear in mind: if the applicant weren't in some way uneasy, he'd never buy insurance. The risk must be there for the surety to be sought and the mere presence of risk is not in itself sufficient reason for rejection of the business.' Do you recall his saying that?"

"No."

"I do, distinctly."

"He never said it."

"He said it forty times a day for forty years."

"What he said was: 'Insurance is the assumption of a calculated risk.' He was, as you probably recall, opposed to conservatism in the acceptance of business. He accepted business that most companies turned down, but it was in no way a gamble with him, except as all of it is a gamble. He brought the calculation of a risk to a science that was way ahead of his time, with a department of investigation that brought in stuff that hadn't even been heard of then. Yet the ratio of his losses was as sound as any in the business. *I'll recommend no risk I can't calculate, and in this case there is concealment.* There is concealment on the part of the beneficiary, of the assured, and I think on the part of the agent."

I flared up but Norton cut me off: "Ed, what is this?"

"I'm stuck on the beneficiary, J. P."

"Mrs. Delavan?"

"I'm going to marry her."

"Is that the matter that's been concealed?"

"No, I wouldn't say so. The main item of concealment is that Mr. Keyes is stuck on the wife of the lady's first husband, but she's *not* going to marry him—and that's what this is all about, though what romance has got to do with the calculation of risk I don't exactly see—though I'm willing to be shown."

I guess it was a dirty crack at Keyes, but I was pretty sore. Norton's mouth began to twitch and I could see he was having a hard time not to laugh. Keyes talked some more, and the trouble with him was that when he got that look in his eye, and told all the times before that he had been right when he smelled something wrong without even knowing what it was yet, he'd shake you, in spite of yourself. Away down deep in me, if I'd told the truth, he shook me, but I was getting bull-headed by then and nothing could change me. He shook Norton, I could see that, for a while we all three sat there, drumming our fingers on our chairs. I called to Linda to put through my New York call.

It was the apartment of a big shot in a company that wanted me bad, and he was standing by, because I'd wired him to. Pretty soon it came through, but it was Norton that picked up the receiver. "He's changed his mind, Linda. Doesn't want the New York call."

I took them to the Palm Room of the Club Fortune, but at eight Norton had to run for his train. He thought it funny Keyes didn't go with him, and as I put him in his cab he asked if there was a little resentment around. "Romance, J. P. has to say goodbye."

"Say, who is the dame?"

"A Mrs. Sperry, I believe her name is."

"Not *Constance?*"

"You know her?"

"Boy, is that a twenty-minute egg!"

"Well, Keyes is carrying it in his Easter basket."

"Ed, you don't know how funny this is. Before she married this Englishman, there were at least six guys that thought they'd grab that fortune, but even they couldn't take it. And now Keyes, the guy that can't be fooled, is plunking a guitar under her window—say, that's a real joke."

When I got back inside, Keyes had kind of

forgotten to be a celebrity for a while, and there seemed to be something on his mind. After a while he said: "Ed, do you think it would be proper for me to call on Mrs. Sperry before I leave, just to say goodbye?"

"Well, why not?"

"You think it would embarrass her?"

"Well, that all depends."

"On what?"

"On what she's told the husband."

"I don't quite understand you, Ed."

"Well, on this earth we got all kinds. Some play around and figure they owe it to themselves on account of how short a time we have here anyhow, and they keep their mouths shut and it sounds wonderful but they've got a way of figuring what they owe themselves is nothing compared to what you owe them, so it's not really quite as wonderful as it sounds. And then there's others that play around, and they figure it's right down sinful of them but they can't help it on account of how wonderful you are, but you better watch them because they've got an unfortunate habit of getting remorse and telling friend husband all, just to square everything up and start over again, and I hear it works but going around to say goodbye depends mainly on the husband. Maybe he wants to shake hands, but on the other hand maybe he's got a Colt automatic and just aching to use it. Personally, if you ask me, I'd kind of give her a ring and see how things stand before I came in range, like you might say."

He sat there with a spoonful of coffee halfway up to his mouth, staring at me like I must be crazy or something. "But, Ed, you don't mean you think there's anything between her and me to tell, do you?"

"You mean you didn't make passes?"

"I wouldn't have thought of it."

"Maybe you missed something."

"Do you mean to make insinuations about her?"

"Hey, hey, hey, be your age."

"But Ed—about *that* woman?"

Well, how do you tell a guy you think his lady friend would go for an insult right on the lipstick? "I was kidding you, Keyes. Just seeing if you could take a rib."

"I'm glad to know it, Ed."

But even with all that said between us, he still wanted to talk, and he opened up about how he thinks he got himself more emotionally involved with her than he had realized, and how he'd hate to leave town without going to see her, because he's pretty sure she feels the same way. Then his face got red again, the way it had in the afternoon, and he kept saying over and over again she was a woman a man could love and not be ashamed of it, and then all of a sudden he was looking over my shoulder at something over near the door. I turned around, and Mrs. Sperry was just coming in with a short, stocky man, and she waved when she saw us. I gave Keyes kind of a kick on his shoe, so he wouldn't look so glum. "It's all right to be in love, but why advertise it?"

"Is he her husband?"

I had the captain do some sleuthing and he came back and said the gentleman was Mr. Richard Sperry. Keyes got glummer, then said: "Look at this."

It was the same old report from the fellow assigned to keep track of her, and he read it again, the description of the man that went into her room and didn't come out: " 'Age, 30-35, height around six feet, weight around 160, hair black with some gray.' Ed, that man's job depends on getting it right. Sperry over there is at least 50, he's not an inch over five feet eight, he can't weigh over 140, and his hair is light red."

"Probably some simple explanation."

"Let's get out of here."

70

I rang Jane and told her I was hooked for the evening, but if I could make it later I'd call her. He and I went over to the hotel, and he said he'd be right down and went upstairs. He was gone quite a while, brushing himself up, he said, and then wanted me to drive him around, so he could think. I took him over into California on the road to Sacramento, and it goes over the Sierras but if it slammed him around a little I didn't really mind. He lit a cigar, then threw it out the window, right in a fire zone. Then he pulled his legs up under him and sat with his heels kind of jammed over against me. So of course that made it nice, trying to drive. He wound down his window, stuck his elbow out, and leaned his chin on it. So of course that made it still better, with a draft blowing down my neck. Then he began clenching and unclenching his left hand, so it rubbed my brake leg. "Cut it out, will you, Keyes? How can I drive with—"

"Quit bothering me."

"Then suppose it wasn't her husband last night?"

"Ed, I'm trying to think.

Sore as I was, the way he rapped it out I didn't have much more to say. I took a peep at him, and something in the way he was staring at those tall trees going by let me see it, just once, whatever it was he had in him that made him the greatest wolf on a phony claim west of the Mississippi River, and maybe the greatest in the business. He wasn't sore, or squint-eyed, or whatever you'd think he would be, trying to dope this out. He was just like a child that asked his mother why something made a noise like it did, and when he got an answer that didn't make sense, he was trying to fit it together. That hurt little frown, with 1,000,000 watts of concentration back of it, was something I've often thought of since. After a while he put down his feet, wound up his window, and said: "Well, I've thought of one angle anyway. Thank God you haven't delivered that policy."

"How do you know what I've done?"

"Don't tell me she's got it?"

"While you were taking your own sweet time brushing up, and considering that when Norton left this was supposed to be signed, sealed and settled, it's highly possible I slipped upstairs on the elevator and handed it to her, just to cheer her up. That could be. A lot of things could be. It would help a lot if you'd disconnect that assumer of yours and stop taking for granted what I do. I'm not under your orders, remember that."

I was pretty disagreeable, and he raved and tore his hair and hooked it up big. I let him run on, maybe encouraged him a little. Of course, I hadn't delivered any policy. I hadn't had a chance for one thing, and I had to figure on it for another thing, what I'd say to her about it. Before the three of us had left the office Norton had O.K.'d it for Linda to deposit Delavan's check, and she'd mailed it out with two or three others, her final job every night, or most nights anyway, as there weren't many days we didn't handle payments. Once we took the money, the policy was legally in force, which was one thing that gave me a pain in the neck about all this delivery stuff Keyes was handing out, because short of a trip to the post office in the middle of the night, and another at daybreak to get the check back, there was no way to stop the thing now. That all-night runaround I wasn't for one second going to start, because all this needed was one more hang-up, and it could land in the soup. At that time, I have to admit, that while I thought I was doing Jane a favor, as I've said, the real thing on my mind was the cup and that $100,000 tilt on my company score. It may have been childish, but in my experience the more childish something is the stubborner you get about it. All this so you get it straight about that policy, and the sweats I went through over it later. I'll try to make clear why I handled it like I did, and I think I'll make sense, but how it stood then, on that ride back from the mountains, was like this: I had it, right in my office safe. It was paid for, and legally we were on the hook. But Keyes supposed, maybe because I deliberately misled him a little, that Jane had it.

He sulked then, and I turned around, and we started back. As we were coming in to Truckee he started up again. "Here, we've got a question of identity. What confused this, from the beginning, was that it was Delavan *himself* who applied for the policy, or appeared to. That made it O.K., even if his reasons were a little screwy, but we're in that kind of business, and if we ever saw a perfect risk, they wouldn't be wanting insurance—old man Norton's pig-iron again. It won't burn down, or fall on somebody, or steal the payroll, or collide with a truck, or blow away, or get hit by lightning, but who wants a policy on it? So all right. But there was one fishy thing about it? *She* opposed the idea. Ed, did you ever see a beneficiary, especially a wife, oppose insurance to mean it? I'm not talking about a little act she puts on. I'm not talking about when she says she can't even bear to think about it, all that stuff. That looks good to the husband, but did she ever turn down a check when the agent takes it around? Not her, my young friend. Once she hears these words, 'Till death do us part,' she's a solid prospect, and when she really goes to town on the other side of the fence, like this girl did, something cooks."

"It does, and I told you what it was."

"Ed, who says that was Delavan?"

What I said to him was nothing, but I'd had hunches about this thing too, as I think I told you. But he didn't wait long. He went right on: "Ask that one question, and it all makes sense. Delavan's in town, I've no doubt of that. He's here, and any question of where he's staying and all the rest of it's all taken care of. He's here for an annulment, and she's in the soup, and he's going to get killed, and all papers on the corpse are going to check up, because it's really going to be Delavan that gets it. But how are we going to prove Delavan's not the man that bought the policy?"

"Can't we appear at the inquest, have a look at the corpse, and testify that he's not?"

"What'll that corpse look like?"

"I haven't the faintest idea."

"But I'm asking you—after, say, an auto accident?"

"Like hamburger, I guess."

"They'll laugh at us, testifying whether it's the guy that bought the policy or who it is. It's six-figure dough to us, and well they know it, and how much our testimony will be worth is exactly nothing at all, especially since even his own mother wouldn't know him."

"However, he's not dead yet."

"He will be. You remember Mrs. Peete?"

"Who?"

"California case. Killed a couple of people."

"Oh, I remember. Kind of got the habit."

"And when she was sentenced to die, she said a peculiar thing to the reporters. She said: 'It is given to all to know the day they were born, but to very few the day they're going to die.' Funny idea, that was, Ed. Kind of reminds you how seldom that moving finger gives out an advance copy of what it's going to write. Well, we've got one. Here were are, two guys in a car, and we know a man named Delavan is due to get it, that a woman is due to collect $100,000 insurance off us, that then she's going to run off with a guy that's been pretending to be the husband, and that we'll have one sweet time finding."

"Listen, Keyes, if your sweetie's been two-timing you that's unfortunate, but don't take it out on me. Or on Delavan. Or on Mrs. Delavan. And don't pull any more of that moving finger stuff. I'm just a little fed up."

"Something funny is going on here."

Chapter 6

Back in Reno we headed for the Club Fortune, where he had forgotten to uncheck his briefcase, on account of being slightly upset when we left there. But we didn't get to the Club Fortune. Because when we started past the hotel there was a terrific jam, with police swinging flashlights and an ambulance parked up Second Street, and I stopped to ask a cop that I knew what had happened. "We don't exactly know yet, Mr. Horner, as we've been trying to save the guy that was standing under the accident when it fell on him—anyway whatever it was that fell on him. A fellow jumped, fell, or dive out of one of the hotel rooms, and he landed on a taxi driver that had just set down a fare, and when the ambulance come we let the first guy lay and had them take *him,* the driver, I mean, but now they've come back I guess we'll be sending the dead one to the morgue and maybe his papers'll show more about it. Them suicides have generally got a note on them, pinned to their coat or somewhere."

Keyes had been sitting there paying no attention, but now he sat up and began to look at the hotel and the ambulance and the crowd, where it was gathered around something on the pavement, and soon as the cop moved off he began to cuss at me in a mean, spiteful way, which was plenty unusual with him, because he was generally polite enough, even when he was setting you crazy with his foolishness. I said: "Well, for the love of Pete and Pete's crazy brother-in-law, Keyes, what is it now?"

"You know what it is, Horner. That's the de luxe tier they're all standing under, the one you tried to get me into, and couldn't, the one she's in. Your little pal. Mrs. Dela-van, that moved fast, once she got that policy. 'Jumped, fell, div'—or was pushed. And here I've got another one of those things on my hands, where whodunit is nothing and *what-was-it* is the whole thing and even when you know it *how-can-you-prove-it* will lick you, and all because you're in love with a no-good trollop I warned you about from the beginning." He looked me in the eye, then, and came out with some stuff I never thought I'd take from any man, and then he opened the door and got out.

At the office I sat staring at the four cups, where they were shining in the light of the desk lamp, trying to figure what I was going to do about that policy, if anything, and what I was going to do about Delavan's check, which was in the mail, on the way to the bank. I could get it, as I've said, by taking one of our office envelopes up to the night window, signing a stop slip, and then in the early morning taking another trip there to claim it. I mean, they require a piece of stationery identical with the piece of mail wanted, and while it was a lot of trouble, it was possible. And I thought a long time. And it kept beating in my head I wasn't going to be cheated out of what I had my mind set on, by Keyes or anybody, just on account of some brainstorm he'd had, *even if it all turned out exactly the way he figured it*. If there'd been fraud, O.K., it wasn't the first time it had happened, and let him prove fraud. That was his job, and if he was so slick at it, he could put us in the clear and get his name in the paper. I might as well put this part right on the line: Somewhere in that cogitation was a guy that made up his mind he was going to take a chance. I wish I could say, that had made up his mind he was going to do what was right come hell or high water. Maybe it was right, I don't know. I've tried to tell myself it was right plenty of times. But why I did it was: I wanted what I wanted, and I was willing to take a chance. Right there was where I skated out where the ice was thin, and it was quite a while before it got thicker, and in between, it got quite a lot thinner.

What I actually did do was put in a call for Jackie, at the Scout ranch, and tell her I was mailing myself a legal paper there, and to hold it for me until I called for it. She was a little short at being waked up, but an important customer was an important customer, so she said O.K. she'd receive it, and put it in a safe place. Then I put the policy in an envelope, stamped it, went over to the post office, and mailed it.

When I rang Jane on the house phone, she sounded nervous and said some police officers were there in connection with something that had been found on the body, and could I call a little later. I sat in the lobby a half hour, and when a couple of cops came out of the elevator I rang her again and she said come up. I was hardly in the room before she was in my arms, holding onto me, not like we'd done before, with romance in it, but like a scared child does when its father comes around. "It did things to me, to hear your voice. The first I heard of it was from the officers, and I felt as though my face and hands had turned to splinters. And then all of a sudden there you were on the line, my big, solid, dependable Ed."

"Thought you might need me."

"After all—he was my husband."

"You can't laugh that off."

"You want a drink, Ed?"

"I could stand one, if coaxed."

"I need something."

She went into the dinette and made a couple of highballs and after we both had a sip she sat down beside me on the sofa and kept holding onto my hand. "They were awfully nice. The officers, I mean. They hadn't wanted to bother me at all, but there was an unmailed letter in his pocket, addressed to me, and they wanted my permission to read it. It seemed they could have anyway, but in that case it would have come out in the papers, and they didn't want me to see it first that way. It was terribly sweet."

"And said?"

"Nothing. Only what had been said before. Over the telephone. About the divorce. But it was friendly. And it shook me up."

It didn't make sense. Because, remember all that Keyes had said was on the assumption that she had the policy. She didn't. It was safely in the U.S. post office, and would be until it was delivered at the Scout the next day, though it was technically in force, if some lawyer told her. And yet there was the dead man, that landed right under her window. And here she was, shaking like a leaf. And here were her hands that felt like ice. I may as well admit it. I never loved her more than I loved her that minute, and never suspicioned her more, either. And the rest of what I've got to tell you, just so you get it all straight and not fall for some fancy stuff

I may put in here and there, to make myself look better, is simply about a guy that kept suspicioning a woman, and getting rid of his hex and then suspicioning her some more, and every time he'd suspicion her he'd fall for her again, until finally he admitted to himself he would go for her no matter what she did, and no matter how much of a heel he had to make of himself to help her do it.

I sat there, trying to square it all up with what Keyes had said, and specially about what he had said about the fellow that told us he was Delavan being nothing but a fake to cover being her lover, when the buzzer rang and when she opened the door that guy, the one I knew as Delavan, walked in. For one second I could feel this throb in the back of my throat, and I wanted to go over and kill them both. But she acted natural, and he said hello to me, and then half took her in his arms. "I'm sorry, Jane. Is there anything I can do?"

"Nothing I can think of."

"You haven't heard anything?"

"About what, Tom?"

". . . Why he did it?"

"He *did* it?"

"Well—I would suppose so."

"I hadn't even thought of that."

"I'm sorry. I just—supposed—"

"That's what the officers meant, wasn't it?"

"They've been here?"

"With his letter he wrote me. But there was *nothing* in it that remotely suggested anything like that. Just a friendly letter. Just—"

"But they—think so too?"

"I guess so."

"I'm sorry I said anything, Jane."

"It's all right."

"Well—if I can do anything."

"I'll let you know."

He went and we sat down again and she lay in my arms with her eyes closed. "That hadn't even once occurred to me. Ed, do you think he did do it? Kill himself, I mean?"

What I said to that I don't know. I held her close, but things were spinning until Keyes rang up. I went in to talk to him and he began apologizing for what he had said. "O.K., Keyes, but what's it all about?"

"It wasn't Delavan that got it."

". . . *What?*"

"It was Sperry."

"Hold on while I drop dead, will you?"

"Amazing, isn't it, Ed?"

84

"Well, Keyes, we all make mistakes."

"Now, Ed, I'm really going to surprise you."

"What, again?"

"I don't feel I've made a mistake."

"O.K., but I've seen Delavan."

"Do you fool with mathematics, Ed?"

"Not if I can help it."

"I do a little. And sometimes, when you've made a gigantic calculation, and you know you've got hold of something that means a lot, you come out with infinity equalling zero, or something like that. Well, so you're crazy, aren't you? Not as a rule you're not. You go back and you check your transformations and you find you came in with a minus px instead of plus, and you make your changes, and all of a sudden there it is, just the way you knew it should be. Ed, I only wish I had something to do with it, beyond the group policy we wrote for the taxi company which I'll have to look into. There's something funny here, and I may say Mrs. Sperry agrees with me."

"Oh, you've seen her?"

"Well, Ed, naturally."

"Well *hey, hey,* this changes things. She's a marriageable widow now."

"Ed, don't be silly!"

"I'm not being silly."

"You're being pretty silly."

"Except, of course, there's the midnight Romeo."

"That's been cleared up. He was a drunken valet of Sperry's. When he came to her with a message, she saw the condition he was in and locked the door to report him to Sperry, who had taken the suite down the hall until the hotel could open up the single in between so they could have the big five-room suite that they wanted. While she was at the phone the valet slipped out on the ledge that runs around the building and popped in one of the corridor windows and out to a gambling place before she could stop him. And I'd like no more references to it."

"O.K., pal."

"And, Ed?"

"Yes?"

"Will you remember what I said. That we both think—"

"Will you kindly go jump in the river?"

It was sweet, all right, to stay late, and hold her in my arms, and feel her tremble a little, because she was a nice girl and if the guy had once been her husband that's how a nice girl ought to feel about it. And yet, driving home, it all came back to me how Keyes had sat there and checked it off about the Moving Finger. We hadn't had an advance copy, but we'd got a whiff of some queer-smelling ink.

Chapter Seven

I keep track of arrivals, and next morning I drove out to the Cinnabar Ranch to tackle three shots from New Jersey that had flown out for some shooting in their private plane. Sometimes, after their first introduction to a Western trail horse, they're not so hard to sell, and I was doing all right. Two of them had no time for me, but the one that was manager of a Newark sheet and tube plant walked over to the stables with me and he didn't say much, but I had that feeling you get, that he was my onion if I peeled him right. I mean, just keep on talking and first thing you know he'll cut in with whatever it is that's on his mind, generally some question about cost. You get out your rate book, and if you're any good you should book him for his medical right there, and next day have his check. So I did and he did, and then I lost him. How, don't ask me. I had him and I didn't have him, and when I got back to the office I knew I wasn't right. It was eating on me a little more than I had thought, whatever it was I wasn't buying about the death of Richard Sperry, geologist. And when Jane rang me, around noon, and asked me to step over, as the police had some questions they wanted to ask her, and she didn't want to be alone with them, Bo-Bo the Butterfly did a couple of fronts in my stomach.

But when they came up to her suite, a patrolman and a sergeant, they treated her fine, and said all they were trying to do was check for their report where he fell from, or jumped from, whatever it was that he did, and they were pretty certain it had to be from his apartment. They hadn't been able to find anybody that saw him fall, but they had questioned everybody on this tier, and three of them had seen him go by the window. But as one of them was the man in the apartment just below hers, it pretty well let any other apartment out, as hers was on the top deck. The sergeant looked at her, then said: "Not to upset you any more than I can help, ma'am, there's things people do when they fall that a police officer knows about and not many other people do, and the way these people tell it sounds O.K. to us, and specially it sounds O.K. the way this fellow just below you tells it. It don't sound to us like stuff he might be making up just to get his name in the paper."

"I don't know what you mean."

"A man falling, he moans. It's a pitiful sound."

"Now I understand."

"These people, that's what they noticed."

"It couldn't have been this suite."

"Were you here?"

"No, that's the point. I was out."

"Where was you, if you don't mind saying?"

"At a picture show."

"Here in town?"

"The Rhythm Parade. At the Granada."

"You come straight here?"

"I arrived at the hotel around a quarter to twelve, after starting down to Harold's and changing my mind and coming here. When I got here the ambulance had arrived and the officers were making the crowd stand back, so I had some trouble getting by. I had no idea what had happened, or who it had happened to, until I got up here and the officers rang me, a few minutes later, and then came up and told me."

"Did this man have a key to your room?"

"Not that I know of."

"He come here often?"

"Never. I hadn't seen him in three years."

"How could he have got in?"

"I don't know."

"He in any trouble that you know of?"

"I know nothing of this recent affairs."

"He sick or anything?"

"He was in good health when he was my husband."

"Get along with his wife?"

"I don't know."

"You got any ideas about this? You understand, ma'am, we're not charging anybody. It's nothing like that. But we got to make a report. It's got to be, the way we figure it, that he went out that window there. The first thing is why, and the next thing is, how."

"I can't imagine his doing a thing like that, or any reason he would have for doing it. Or how he could get in here, or why."

"That window's high, for one thing."

"Didn't he have a window of his own?"

"He had a wife of his own, too. Watching him, maybe."

"One reason for suicide, no doubt."

That's what she said, but she kind of snapped it out and everybody laughed. After a minute she laughed. It was easy to see that the cops had put it together on a suicide basis, with some trouble going on between Sperry and Mrs. Sperry as the reason for it. Then the sergeant said: "Anybody else in the apartment at the time you was out?"

"No. . . . Or, wait. I'll see."

She went in the bedroom and picked up the telephone. There was some talk and she came back. "I just happened to think that my maid may have been up, putting out my things for the night."

"Had they been put out when you got in?"

"Yes, of course."

"She coming?"

"She's on her way up."

So that was the third time I saw this Harriet Jenkins that you probably read about, but the first time I really had a good look at her. She was about the sloppiest-looking thing in the way of a woman I ever saw, and cheap, and 100% servant girl from the cap on her head to the shoes on her feet. But if you have some little trouble understanding what came out later, I may as well tell you she was just about as sexy a number as you're liable to see in a month of looking. She looked maybe twenty-six or -eight, and her face was coarse, her hair ratty red, and her neck that certain color that made you wonder how often she washed. But don't let anybody tell you that under the ten-cent-store makeup, the cotton stockings, the bombazine uniform there wasn't looks, shape and a way of handling her gum. There was also a droopy way of handling her eyes.

She came in with her own key and stopped when she saw the cops and shot a look at Jane like she wanted a cue. But Jane just said they wanted to ask her a few questions and told her she could sit down. Sitting down didn't seem to be something she was very good at, anyway around Jane, but she pulled the chair out from in front of the writing desk, sat on the edge of it, pulled her dress down over her knees, and began looking from one to the other of everybody in the room. That went on for quite some time, because cops, they make a specialty of sitting there looking at you, so you get fidgety wondering what they're thinking. But the sergeant got enough of it and sounded off: "You knew Mr. Richard Sperry?"

"Oh, yes, sir. 'E was my employer for some years."

"When's the last time you seen him?"

She looked away and kind of huddled up like some puppy dog that was getting a bawling out, and then she asked Jane: "Is it important, ma'am?"

"Quite important."

" 'E asked me not to say."

"I'd tell it, if I were you."

" 'E gave me a tenner not to say."

"Regardless of what he gave you, it's desirable that you tell anything you know, and it may have very bad consequences, particularly to *yourself,* if you conceal anything you know. The police officer has asked you when was the last time you saw Mr. Sperry."

"It was last evening, sir."

"Where?"

" 'Ere."

"In the hotel?"

"In this room."

"When?"

"Around eleven, sir."

The cops looked at each other and Jane looked at me and then remembered not to look at me, and you could tell this was something nobody had expected. But the maid didn't seem to think there was anything out of the way about it. "He came here looking for Mrs. Delavan?"

" 'E did, twice."

"Tell us about it."

"The first time was around nine. I was

lying down on the spare bed, 'aving a look at the illustrated magazines, as Mrs. Delavan was seeing a picture and there was no need for me to 'urry my work in any way. And the buzzer sounded and I got up and put on my cap and peeped out the pigeon 'ole, as they call it 'ere. And 'oo should be in the 'all but Mr. Sperry. And I welcomed 'im in, for I 'adn't seen im since I left Bermuda. And 'e was most gracious to me, as we 'ave one or two personal memories, I think I may say. But 'e was deeply disappointed when I told 'im Mrs. Delavan would be late getting in, and shortly after that 'e left. And it was at this time that 'e gave me the tenner and asked me not to mention 'is visit to anybody. 'E repeated 'imself several times. 'Don't misunderstand me, Jenkins,' 'e said. 'Tell nobody. *Nobody.* ' "

"And who was nobody?"

"Mrs. Sperry, I think sir, but 'e made no exceptions."

"And this was a little after nine?"

" 'Is first visit, yes, sir. Then, around eleven I'd say it was, 'e came again. I invited 'im in to wait for Mrs. Delavan, and 'e began walking up and down 'ere, very nervous like, and often looking out the window for 'er, and leaning out and looking down at the

94

street, until I 'ad to warn 'im it was dangerous as 'e could lose 'is balance and fall. Then 'e calmed down a little and I suggested 'e might prefer to wait for 'er alone. So I left 'im there, and left word with him for Mrs. Delavan I would remain dressed a little while if she needed me, and around twelve, as there was no call, I went to bed."

"Well, that about clears it up."

The sergeant said that to the patrolman, and the patrolman opened a portable typewriter he had beside him and stuck a piece of paper in and started to write. But Jane got up, lit a cigarette, and broke in on it. "Not quite . . . Jenkins, why have you let a whole morning go by without telling me this?"

"Ma'am, 'e asked me not to. 'E gave me a tenner."

"Doesn't it seem to you that under all the circumstances you've been carrying discretion a little too far?"

"I've accepted your suggestion, ma'am, to conceal nothing from the officers, but if I may say 'ow I feel, I'm not looking forward at all to my next meeting with Mr. Sperry, and it'll cost me the tenner, I'll 'ave you know, in connection with all your fine ethical ideas, for I can 'ardly keep it now I've broken the promise I made to him."

95

". . . Jenkins, haven't you *heard?*"

"I've not been out, ma'am. I've been in my room all morning after making myself a cup of coffee, waiting for your call."

"I didn't ring you—I didn't want to talk about it. . . . Mr. Richard was killed shortly after you left him last night, in a fall from that very window."

"Oh, no, ma'am, don't tell me that!"

After the cops went and Jenkins quit her bawling, it was Jane that cracked up a little, and it took some little cheek-patting to get her calmed down. But when the phone rang I wouldn't let her answer. I figured it was the reporters, and if she was that much upset to find out Sperry had had something friendly in mind when he came up there, I didn't think facing a bunch of buzzards and lead pencils and notebooks would do her much good. We let the phones ring and I put on her coat and zipped her down to the basement and out the side way to my car and headed out of town with her and I had no idea where we were going, but we wound up at Sacramento. We had a swell dinner at the Senator and at last it seemed everything was cleared up and coming back she tucked her hand in mine and said she was falling in love, I said O.K. by me. She said O.K. by her. It's funny the dumb things you say that mean so much to you you could remember them the rest of your life.

We got in late, and it must have been after two o'clock when my phone rang and on the line was Keyes. "Ed, have you seen the papers?"

"About that maid?"

"That's what I mean."

"No, but I was there when she talked to the cops."

"Does it strike you as peculiar?"

"She hadn't heard it. She hadn't been out."

"You know anything about English servants?"

"I don't keep servants."

"Neither do I, but young Norton's always got three or four of them around, and now and then I go out there. Ed, they're the most gossipy, curious breed of people I ever saw, and how that maid, with romance waiting upstairs, could sit there in her room without ever once ringing Mrs. Delavan's phone I simply don't see."

"What romance?"

"The former husband."

"I'm the romance in that household."

"Yeah, but does the maid know it?"

"I wouldn't be surprised."

"Ed, it won't add up. The former husband shows up, hands her a ten-spot to keep her mouth shut, and on the second trip she leaves him there to wait for his former wife who's her mistress. I'm telling you, she couldn't wait to find out what it was all about. Her nose would be quivering for it. And yet she didn't make one move to go after it—that is, if the papers have got it right. Or have they?"

"On that point, apparently they have."

"Well, thank God it's not my grief."

"Mine either."

"This is one time we can spectate."

"That's it. Just take it easy."

Part Three:
The Willing
Widow

Chapter Eight

The inquest was next night at a mortuary on Sixth Street, and Jane wasn't a witness, but the cops had asked her to attend, as something might come up, and they wanted her there in case. So we drove the maid over, and Keyes was already there, with Mrs. Sperry, a big-shot lawyer in town named Morton Lynch, and a squinty-eyed number named Biggs that kept fingering a trick derby he had, that seemed to be Sperry's valet, and that corresponded, in looks at least, to the guy named in the eye's report on who didn't come out of the room that night. Mrs. Sperry was in black, with a veil, but one you could see through. She didn't look at Jane or the maid, but after we had sat down she nodded at me with a sad little smile, and reached over and gave my hand a grip. Some newspaper men were there, with three or four other guys that weren't newspaper men but tried to look like they were. They work for the adjusters, so I knew there was an insurance angle. Some cops were at a table, and on the other side of a counter was the undertaker, but back there on a table you could see part of a sheet, with something under it. The whole room wasn't much bigger than my private office, and we all sat on folding chairs that had been set up in rows with an aisle down the middle. Every time somebody would come in they'd start to sit in the first two rows on the right-hand side, but the cops would wave them to other seats. It turned out, when some more cops came in with them, where they'd been rounding them up, these two rows were for the jury.

The coroner was Dr. Hudson, that I had met once or twice, and the cops all stood up when he came in. He was a squatty little guy, and after he had sat down and taken some papers out of his briefcase and studied them, the same sergeant as had come to see Jane banged on the table with the flat of his hand for us to stop talking. Then he asked all who had been summoned to testify to raise their right hands and the maid did and quite a few others did and he gave them the oath to tell the truth, the whole truth and nothing but the truth, and they all mumbled they would. Then he called the maid and the valet to view the body and when they had he asked them if they knew the deceased and they said they did and he was Richard

Sperry and lived on the island of Bermuda. Then he asked if there was anybody else who wished to view the body, corroborate the identification, contest it, or add anything to this part of the inquest, and he looked at Mrs. Sperry, but she shook her head no and put her handkerchief to her eyes. Then he had two cops tell how they had got the call in their car, and all the rest of it, how it had happened that night, anyway from their end of it. Then the ambulance doctor that had certified the death testified. Then two autopsy doctors went on, and they told a lot of compound occipital stuff, but all it seemed to add up to was that he died of a bashed-in head. Then he had a huddle with the sergeant and called the maid. She told it about like she had told it to the cops. Then he looked around and asked if anybody else had any knowledge of the case. He didn't expect any answer, you could tell that, because he was already putting his papers back in the briefcase. And Keyes didn't either, you could tell from the way he was whispering to Lynch. And his head couldn't have snapped around quicker if a gun had been fired in his ear than it did when Mrs. Sperry rose up like a ghost coming out of the floor, stepped into the aisle, did a slow march to

103

the chair, they had put out for the witness, and said: "I have."

"You know something of this, Mrs. Sperry?"
"I do."
"Something more than you told the police?"
"I told the police only the barest facts—that I spent the evening in my suite, that I was not with my husband at the time he met his tragic end, and that I had nothing more to tell them."
"You mean, other things have come to light since?"
"I mean there was more."
"That you—withheld?"
"I had to know my legal position first."
"In respect to?"
"Self-destruction."
"I don't quite understand you."
"In this country, what do we call it?"
"Suicide, I suppose you mean."
"In England, only the insane commit suicide."
"I'm not following you at all."
"Others, and my husband was as sane as you are, commit *felo de se,* which under English law is a criminal act."
"Mrs. Sperry, we're holding this inquest in America."

"The estate, however, will be settled in Bermuda."

"Is the estate involved, Mr. Lynch?"

"I would say, yes."

"You mean the insurance, on a suicide clause?"

"I'm not talking about insurance. There is no insurance, payable to Mrs. Sperry at any rate, that we know of. I'm not prepared to give an opinion at the drop of a hat as to how much the estate is involved under English law in a case where the deceased took his own life. All I know is, if the verdict here tonight is rendered that way, it is possible the estate will automatically become the estate of a criminal, which may be, for all I know, administered differently in England from the estate of other persons. And in the case of Mr. Richard Sperry, part of the estate will be copyrights on valuable technical works, which may be forfeited, as it is highly possible a criminal in England is not entitled to copyright. This is a field too tricky for an American attorney to make any impromptu assumptions about. I should like to say that as her counsel I have advised Mrs. Sperry she is not required to give, and in my opinion shouldn't give, any evidence in regard to this, of any kind, for a wife cannot be compelled to testify to her husband's crime—"

"In this country it's not a crime."

"Pardon me, it may be held, in the property jurisdiction, to be a crime."

"She is not compelled, naturally, to testify."

"But I'm *going* to testify."

"What is it you have to tell, Mrs. Sperry?"

"I saw my husband leap to his death."

They'd been having it back and forth, not too hot, more or less friendly, and everybody was kind of interested, because all that English stuff was new to them, but now if a nest of hornets had been kicked over in the middle of the floor they couldn't have set up a louder buzz than went around when she said that. The sergeant banged with his hand again, and they got quiet, but the quick way one of the reporters slipped out of the room showed what a sensation it was. The coroner stared at her and said: "You were with him at the time? Contrary to what you told the police?"

"I was where I told them I was. In my suite."

"Please continue, Mrs. Sperry."

"I was sitting by my window, very depressed."

"At—anything relevant to this case?"

"At my husband's talk about ending his life."

"He'd been talking that way?"

"Often."

"Yes, but lately?"

"That night."

"Did he have some reason?"

"None, none at all."

"But there must have been *something.* "

"He said, when we came upstairs after dinner, 'It is a very curious thing. Here I am, a man to be envied. I am successful, I have been recognized generously by the country I claim as my own, I have a beautiful wife, I love her, I am loved in return. I have everything to live for. But your true suicide type finds his own reasons. The time will come when I'll do this thing . . .' His reasons never made sense, at least to me. And yet, perhaps all the more for that reason, I felt he was warning me."

She took out her black handkerchief, wiped her eyes, and went on: "I don't know how long I sat there. He had gone out some time before. A little *before* nine, as I recall. Then I noticed something above me. Above me and across from me, on the street side of the hotel. A man appeared at the window and leaned out. I couldn't see who it was, but it seemed to me he was acting most peculiarly. Then he climbed out and sat there, with his feet dangling outside, and stared down at the street—"

"Wait a minute. At Mrs. Delavan's window?"

"I don't know her window."

"You're in the south wing?"

"Yes, on the seventh floor."

"Facing the setback?"

"My sitting room does."

"Then your suite, on that side, looks across to hers."

"I suppose so. How long this took, I don't know. It seemed ages, but I imagine it was no more than a few seconds. I had some horrible premonition who it was, and jumped up to open the window and call. I have some recollection of the window sticking, but I can't be sure. The man jumped. He braced his hands against the sill, and jumped. From then on, I have no recollection of anything until I woke up on the floor, deathly sick. How long I had been there I don't know. I got up, went to the bathroom to bathe my face in cold water, then went to the bedroom. Then the phone rang. It was the police, asking if they could come up."

"And then you withheld what you knew?"

"Not intentionally, at first."

"What actually did you tell them?"

"What they asked of me: Who I was, how long I had been in Reno, where I had spent the evening. It wasn't until they had been there some little time that it dawned on me they hadn't any idea of what had happened— except, of course, conjecturally. I mean, they still didn't know which suite he had jumped from—or 'fallen,' as they always added, I think to spare my feelings. And then it occurred to me that perhaps nobody except myself had seen him. People don't as a rule go about staring at the top floor of a hotel at that hour of night. Then it was, and then only, that I decided to say nothing to them until I had engaged counsel."

"They told you he'd been in the bar?"

"I believe they did."

"You didn't think it funny he'd gone up there?"

"Up where? I didn't know whose room it was."

"You have no idea what he was doing there?"

"I'm content to believe he had his reasons."

"I guess that's about all."

"One other thing, Doctor."

"Yes, Mr. Lynch?"

"I think you owe it to her, as she seems to want full weight and credence given to her evidence here, and in no way regards it as a subjective matter, I mean she wouldn't be satisfied with merely getting it off her chest, as they say—to instruct this jury, before it considers its verdict, that her delay in disclosing what she saw in no way impeaches her credibility. She was not required to testify, or tell the police anything."

"Mr. Lynch, why don't you tell them?"

"Then by me, the jury is so informed."

"Mrs. Sperry, may I raise a point that you could clear up, but that would have more to do with the question of credence than all the law Mr. Lynch knows, though I don't doubt he knows a lot. Why do you disregard him and tell it anyway?"

"Out of respect for the truth."

"Even if the estate is involved?"

"A clear conscience comes first."

You could tell by the looks on their faces after they came out of the back room that the jury was going to give her a break on all that legal stuff. The verdict was that he died from the effects of a fall, caused "in a manner unknown to this jury."

Chapter Nine

I was out on the street, waiting for Jane, while she stood by with the maid on some stuff the cops had to wind up, and I had taken quite a few turns up and down the block before I noticed Keyes around the corner, staring at the river with that same look in his eyes he'd had that night in the car, before Sperry was killed. I strolled over, and it was a minute or two before he said: "Ed, when somebody dies, you deliver the indemnity check in person?"

"Oh, always."

"On a suicide case, how does the woman act?"

"The widow?"

"How does she take it?"

"Well, she's generally upset. Naturally."

"They just hate it."

"Well, who does love an undertaker?"

"That's not quite it. What they feel is not grief. It's resentment. Maybe they keep quiet about it, as a matter of pride. But they've got that look in their eye. They regard it as an insult, a reflection on the marriage, and especially a reflection on themselves. . . . Did you get anything like that in there?"

"I thought she behaved with great dignity."

"But how much bitterness did she show?"

"I didn't notice any."

"Nor I either. I've been with her now for a considerable part of two whole days, and I've been struck by her complete freedom from rancor. She's cracked up a few times, but there have been no hard feelings, and in fact when I've called her attention to one or two peculiar things about it she's always come back with something that showed she preferred to regard it as an accident. Now tonight she says she saw it happen, and kept it concealed for legal reasons—but they were exactly the kind of reasons she would have placed before me, if it all took place as she says it did. Furthermore, it wouldn't be possible for a woman to live a week or more in the same hotel as her husband's former wife, and not know where her room was. Furthermore, even without law, or possible insurance angles, no member of a family ever admits anything that spells suicide. That's one thing they'll do anything to keep under cover, to pretend didn't happen. And in my experience, I've never known an exception: if they do seem to come out in the open, it's to cover something up."

". . . Such as?"

"Whatever she really saw."

"Spit it out, Keyes. What are you getting at?"

"Ed, Lynch said there was no insurance angle, but we know there is, from the investigators that attended this inquest. But we don't know what those investigators, if they were to stay on the case, might turn up. The quickest way to get rid of them, if there's a suicide clause in effect somewhere, would be to place sworn testimony on the record of a public inquest that establishes an eyewitness. That closes the case—for the cops, who are concerned only with violations of the law, and for these buzzards, that are concerned with everything, up and down the line, that affects a claim . . . Ed, I confess this disturbs me."

"Your lady love fibbing on you, you mean?"

"It's shifty. And I've been—"

"Kind of stuck on her?"

"I may as well admit it. . . . And yet—if

she's covering up for *his* good name, to conceal some sort of scandal she knew had to come out, if this thing were really investigated—"

"She'd still be your perfect lady."

"That's it. And she is a thoroughbred, we know that."

"At least, if she was a horse, we'd *know* it."

"And that girl, that Mrs. Delavan—"

"Oh, so *she's* the scandal!"

"Well, after all, it was her room, and she was his former wife."

I didn't clip him on the jaw, you'll probably be surprised to learn, but later that night I was to hear about insurance again. It was in Jane's suite, and she had her head on my shoulder, and was relaxed and friendly, because, as she said, "I could never bring myself to take pleasure in the death of another human being, but I can't forget either that this writes *finis* to one of the most ghastly chapters of my life. I had nothing to do with Dick's decision, have no idea of the reason for it. Just the same, he's gone. It's the end. I'm not glad, but for the first time in a long, long while, I'm at peace."

Then the phone rang.

I paid no attention, lit a cigarette while she went in the bedroom to answer. But she was gone some little time, and when she came back she said: "What could he have meant? 'Do something about the insurance?' "

"Who was he?"

"Ireland, I think he said."

". . . He's a go-between. For insurance companies."

"But—there *is* no insurance."

"There has to be, if he rang you."

"There was, but the policies lapsed."

"Do you still have them?"

"They're in Kennebunkport."

"Maine?"

"My family was there when I came back from Bermuda. We have a summer place there. It had been years since I had banking connections in New York, so I put them in a safe deposit box there. Then we came back on Labor Day and I couldn't get them, or my other stuff that was with them. It didn't seem to make much difference, as we expected to be back in the fall, for skiing. But various things came up. And then there began this wrangle with Dick, by mail, over the policies. He wanted to change the beneficiary, to this woman, I suppose, but to do it he had to have the policies. But I simply was not going to take a special trip to Maine for some insurance policies to be made out to a woman reeking with money already, and one that I owed not one bit of consideration to, believe me. Then the last letter I got from him said most curtly that he was going to have the policies cancelled. Or let them lapse, I guess that was it."

"Did he do it?"

"Well, did he? I haven't heard from him since."

"He was a fool if he did."

"Why?"

"You got insurance, you've got it. You lose it you don't know where you stand. You've got to pass another medical examination, you'll pay a higher premium, as you've got older all the time, and there's always the risk you can't pass the examination. He probably kept them up. You'll cash in—that is, unless—"

"Unless what?"

"The suicide clause touches you out."

"On that they could refuse to pay?"

"If it's still in effect. When were these policies written? Before your marriage with Sperry broke up, I would assume."

"There were several. The smaller ones, totalling twenty-eight hundred dollars, I think, were written about five years ago. But the big one, for twenty-five thousand, was taken out a little less than two years ago.

"Those clauses generally run for two or three years."

"Ed, I suddenly have a horrible suspicion. That's why she said what she did. Just now, at the inquest. Ed, did it strike you that was a most unlikely tale? Possibly not, as you didn't know him. Of all things you could believe about him, that would be the last. . . . And yet why would she lie about it just to keep me out of money? Is she that vindictive about me?"

"Taking an awful risk, too."

"I would think so. . . . What do I do now?"

"Get the policies."

"I can't."

"You'll have to."

"I'll have to go to Maine in person, and I can't leave Reno. I'll lose my residence if I do, and have to begin all over again."

"O.K., begin over again, but get them."

"But it'll be six more weeks, and—"

"And the rest of your life. What do you care?"

"I hadn't thought of that."

"O.K., think about it."

"With you, is that the idea?"

"Something like that."

I went down around twelve, and in the lobby Keyes was waiting for me. I started by, because he'd got under my skin with what he had said, but then I thought oh well, he makes everybody hate him so why act like he knew any better. I wasn't any too agreeable about it, though, when I asked him what he wanted, and I took my time about it when he asked me to sit down. He took out a fountain pen and held it out for me to look at. "You'd be surprised where that came from."

"I never saw it before."

"Nor I, Ed. The bartender gave it to me."

"He never gave me a gold pen."

"To give Mrs. Sperry."

"Likes her?"

"It was turned in. It belongs to Sperry, and as I'd been seen with her quite a lot, they thought I wouldn't mind seeing that she got it. He had lent it to somebody that wanted to write down the title of one of his books and neglected to give it back before he went upstairs. It seems there was a call that night from Mrs. Sperry to the bartender. Asking him to remind Sperry not to forget his engagement with the little lady that was waiting upstairs."

"Who, for instance?"

"She didn't say. The bartender reminded Sperry and he went."

"O.K., Keyes, but why hasn't the bartender told it?"

"Why should he? It ties in with what he's seen in the papers, and who would get mixed up with something unless he had a reason to? So far as he knows, it means nothing. We know that it does. Something went on that night that she wants bottled up, and so far she's got it her way."

"At Jane's expense, you might say."

"How so?"

"How do you think? The suicide clause naturally."

"Oh, so there *is* insurance?"

"Turns out there is."

"Now it makes sense."

"Hey, you! On a bartender's say-so—"

"But, Ed, why would he make this up? Besides, I've already checked on it. The girl on the switchboard, when I said I was trying to trace ownership of a pen, and asked if she remembered any call to the cocktail bar around eleven night before last, had it right away; Mrs. Sperry wanted to speak with Alec, and she got him for her. Alec is the bartender and it was he who handed me the pen."

"Is this your case?"

"In a way, yes."

"I didn't know we were on the risk."

"Ed, I've told you, there's something I've got to know. If she's covering something she's involved in, it would be a blow, I admit it. It would—make a difference. But if she's covering for somebody else, frankly I'd consider it magnificent."

"Covering what, for instance?"

"Murder, perhaps."

"But nothing serious?"

"Scandal, pretty definitely."

I think I've told you, he kind of gets on people's nerves. You'd like to knock his block off, but for some reason you don't. He got this dreamy look in his eyes, and said: "We know now, pretty definitely, what the scandal was and who it was. The phone call proves Mrs. Sperry knew about it. It's beginning to tie up."

Chapter Ten

I spent half the night lying awake, with that same old creepy feeling coming over me, because there was the phone call and there was the insurance, and you couldn't laugh them off. Next day the papers were full of the inquest, with "wealthy American baring facts of English husband's fatal fall," and I kept waiting for it, whatever it was that was about to pop. And then everything died down, and you'd think there'd never been a guy named Richard Sperry, or a fatal fall, or anything. Jane flew east for the policies, got them, flew back, put her claim in. On the smaller ones she was O.K. and collected. On the big one the suicide clause still had a month to run, and she hadn't a Chinaman's chance, at least as it looked then, but I told her to put a claim in anyway. She started her period of residence all over again, and the Count's education all over again too, with me at the edge of the track looking on, and Jackie getting that gleam in her eye, over what she said was the prettiest show ring entry she'd ever had at the ranch. Delavan was mildly upset at the residence period having to be started all over again, but not as much as we would have expected. The day after the autopsy, or pretty soon anyway, Keyes crossed me up by going home. I had thought he was really going to bear down and try to marry that pile of money. La Sperry, I mean. But he went home and stayed home. It came late fall, and I picked out a Christmas present for Jane, a gold cigarette case I thought she'd like. I had it gift-wrapped and tucked it away in my desk.

And then one day she and I were headed for a ride and were going down in the hotel elevator when a bellboy got on with a little fox terrier with a blanket on her underneath the leash harness. Jane no sooner saw her than she gave a yelp and took her in her arms, and come to find out, it was Sperry's dog and her name was Dolly. But if the dog had ever seen her before she gave no sign of it. All she did was mope, and the boy said she'd been like that since Sperry died. "If something's not done, Mrs. Delavan, I don't think she's going to be around much longer."

"Perhaps I can help."

"Gee, if you only would."

So we fixed it up she was going to exercise the little thing, and when she got done she'd bring him back to the lobby, and the boy seemed to get it she didn't want any truck with Mrs. Sperry. But a wink passed, and they fixed it up the exercising would be done on the roof. "That's one thing I learned from Dick. If you're in a hotel and you have a dog on your hands, the roof's closer than the street, and a great deal simpler."

The roof was just a jumble of vents, chimneys, and water tank, with a boardwalk promenade for the sun-tanners and badminton nets and shuffle board stuff and patio furniture. We walked Dolly around and how far we got cheering her up was nowhere. After a while we sat down and Jane took the dog in her lap and tried talking to her. And then all of a sudden she said: "What's *she* doing here?"

"Who? Mrs. Sperry?"

"Yes. I thought she'd left."

"Does she *have* to be doing something?"

"She doesn't live here."

"Maybe she just likes Nevada."

"And what's *he* doing here? Tom?"

"Well, you're getting a divorce, aren't you?"

"*I'm* getting a divorce. He came out here to get an annulment, and now he's changed his mind. I'm to file a suit which he's not going to contest, and there's no reason whatever, no legal reason I can think of, for him to stay on here."

"Maybe he just *says* he's changed his mind."

"I'm sure he's not crossing me."

"Well, it's nothing to us."

It popped in my mind about the phone call to the bartender, which I had never told her about, because it could have meant her. But now she seemed 100% on the up-and-up and I heard myself open up about it. "Ed, why haven't you said something about this before?"

". . . I thought it might upset you."

"You mean you thought I did have some sort of engagement with Dick?"

"I mean I was sick of him."

"But I hadn't seen him in three years."

"So you told me."

"And I was at a picture show."

"Yes, I know."

"But—I still don't understand it. I'm sure the bartender told Mr. Keyes exactly what you say he did, and that it happened that way, but—it doesn't sound like her—or anybody. To send a message through a bartender instead of asking for Dick and talking to *him*. And what he did next, coming to my room, and having that long palaver with Jenkins. He was kind to servants, but awfully short-spoken. That he should have let down his hair the way he did, or she says he did, is almost incredible. It all seems so strange."

By that time the dog was so restless she

did nothing but moan and twist and wriggle on Jane's lap. Jane handed her to me, went and got a cord off one of the badminton nets, and tied one end of it to the leash and the other to a table leg. Then she gave the little dog a pat and told her to run around. The dog didn't wait, or even look at us. She gave a little whimper, raced for the parapet, and jumped. I dived for the cord and missed, but the table leg held it, and in a second I was hauling in a pooch that was scared so bad, and bopped so bad, where she whammed against the wall outside when the cord tightened, that she clean forgot she was supposed to be torching for somebody, and was so glad when I held her to me it was comical. But when I went over to Jane with her all I got was a stare. "Ed, do you know what's under that spot where she jumped?"

I looked, and what I was looking at was the place on the pavement where they picked up Sperry. "Ed, this is directly over that window of mine that Constance Sperry said she saw him jump from. The little lady he had the engagement with is right there in your arms, and he had a standing date with her every night— every night they were together, that is—since he bought her in Venezuela five years ago. She was here, she saw it happen, and that's why she leaped into what, so far as her little mind could understand, was his grave. Ed, after a phone call to the bartender, made in such way that it must have been intended to implicate me in something she knew was about to happen, and after what we've just seen, there's only one thing to believe. They brought Dolly up, they started walking around, she stopped to admire the view or something. He stopped beside her. Then a quick push, and with that low parapet almost anything would cause him to lose his balance. Then a beeline to her room to take the call from the police she knew would come."

"Seems funny they weren't seen."

"Who would see them?"

"Elevator girl. Anybody."

"But you don't know hotels, perhaps. They don't like dogs taken up on the roof. Didn't you see the wink the boy gave me just now, as I slipped him his dollar? And Dick always used the stairway, where they would meet *nobody* that hour of night. And the phone call, which would mean one thing to Dick and another thing to the bartender, and the place she picked out to do it, would throw suspicion on me if any suspicion arose, because she must have known about those insurance policies. Suicide, though, that was safer. The frame-up against me she didn't really expect to fall back on unless she absolutely had to."

"But what would she kill him for?"

"Let me think."

So she thought. After a long time she said: "Maybe I have it now.

"It makes no sense to me."

"Dick probably wanted the marriage to go on. Perhaps she didn't."

"How do you figure this out?"

"The way she acted with Tom. Complimenting him when he told her about that insurance he tried to take out for me. I took that for just a little preliminary soft soap, though the real scheme would be disclosed later. Then when Dick threatened Tom, it all fitted together and I took it for granted the two Sperrys were a team. But if she was up to something Dick didn't know about, if she's found somebody she likes better—"

"Like Keyes?"

"I think she's kidding Keyes."

"Go on."

"If she was up to something Dick would never have stood for, then Tom's annulment action was the one perfect break for her. It would be granted, it would almost certainly lead to the Bermuda court rescinding Dick's divorce, and her marriage would then, of course, be automatically annulled. She'd be out, she'd never have to face anything up with Dick, and best of all, there'd be nothing to decide about property or anything of that sort, and remember she's the one that has the money. But when Dick scared Tom out of it, that popped everything into the soup. So, do something quick. So, phone call. So, get him above my window. So, bump him."

"Keyes thought she was scared to death of the insurance investigators, and what they might find out. He figured she made it suicide, so they'd close the case and go home.

"Then he thinks she did it?"

". . . He thinks you did."

"*I?* Are you serious?"

"He is. And if he is, it is."

"But why would I do it?"

"Insurance. Spite."

"Over what?"

"Sperry marrying her."

"Then Mr. Keyes must be crazy."

"About darling Constance he is."

We went over it some more, and the more we went over it the more it made sense. She kept going back to the swim in Bermuda, when she was sure he meant she wasn't coming back, and said he was never like that until he met Mrs. Sperry. Then that got her started on Jenkins, and then she said: "But Ed, why was *she* in on it?"

"You sure she was?"

"If it happened up here she was lying."

"Keyes thought her story was peculiar."

"But *why?* She didn't even like Constance Sperry. After I left, she did nothing but write me what a hell on earth it was working for her, and pleading with me to take her back and bring her to the United States. And it wasn't until I found out her mother had been a waitress on the Aquitania and she was actually born in New York that it was possible to, get her in, but those letters, believe me, were pitiful."

"When was this?"

"Last month."

"Then she didn't come to this country with you?"

"Under the law, she couldn't."

When we went down she rang Jenkins and told her to come up. "Wait a minute, Jane. I'm not sure I'd tip what you know until we've got this better figured out than we have. I wouldn't say anything to her. Not now."

"Say something to her? I'm going to fire her."

"No! You're forgetting something!"

"I don't think so."

"Your big policy. Your $25,000."

"What does she have to do with it?"

"If he didn't do it, and you didn't, you're due to get paid. And if we can sweat it out of Jenkins who did do it, you better keep her here till we're ready with the heat, and she'll be where you want her instead of some place else."

"I'll do no more about the insurance."

"*What?*"

"*I must have an end of this!*"

She had the beat-up look around the eyes, and was already at the writing desk, making out a check for Jenkins' pay. So she went through on it, the dumbest thing that was done in connection with the whole case. Jenkins stood there, and kept asking if there was something she had done, and couldn't she have some explanation, or another chance. Jane kept saying she'd decided on another arrangement, and pretty soon Jenkins left. It seemed to me, watching her, that she was talking more to watch Jane than to hang onto her job.

That night when I got home there was a message to ring Operator 22, or whatever the number was, in Los Angeles. When she put me through it was Keyes. "Ed, the Reno police have that phone call to the bartender."

"How do you know?"

"They rang me."

"Why you?"

"To see what I knew. After all, I'd been with Mrs. Sperry a lot, and I delivered the pen."

"And what did you say?"

"That it was the first I had heard of it."

"Then that lets you out."

"Ed, I'm warning you."

"Thanks."

"Keep away from that dame."

"You coming up here?"

"I might fly. Over the week-end."

"About the taxi driver or Mrs. Sperry?"

"Oh, the driver recovered."

"Drop in. I may have news."

Chapter Eleven

So he flew up here, just about the time the cops began giving Jane a working over that got worse from day to day. First they'd ask to come over, she'd ask me to stand by, then they'd go over it some more, where she was that night, when was the last time she'd seen Sperry, and they'd spring trap questions on her until a couple of times I had to kick their shins to make them get back over the line. That's bad with a cop, to act like there's anything you're afraid to be questioned about, and to have a boy friend around a woman to tell her how to talk. But with that look in her eyes, I wasn't sure how much she could take. They'd go, and next day they'd be back, and you could tell they'd been talking to Mrs. Sperry, but what she'd told them you couldn't tell, because if there's one thing a cop is good at its keeping his own mouth shut and letting you do the talking. All you could say for it was that the papers didn't have it, so at least it could have been worse.

But when Keyes arrived, and finally did get around to dropping by the office, I found out what Mrs. Sperry had told them. The point was she was trying, or pretending to try to cover up for Jane, but since it was her own phone call, she had to put it on the line who it was Sperry was supposed to have the date with. She said Sperry had told her there was a "little old lady," who "lived upstairs in the hotel somewhere," and "wanted to ask him some questions about Bermuda," if he "would drop by at the end of the evening, before he went to bed." And it seems the cops thought there was something funny about it, all of it, especially the little old lady, and the funny hours she kept, and the funny coincidence they couldn't find any little old lady. "But she was ready for them, Ed. Do you know what she told them?"

"Something good, I bet."

"That she didn't believe it either."

"Well, say, that *is* good."

"That it seemed so fishy, and that was what made her so depressed. She was certain the story about the little old lady was just an excuse of Sperry's to get out."

"Funny she reminded him though Keyes."

"That was to check on him."

"That he was in the bar?"

"On a drinking deck, not a jumping deck."

"Why did she practically beg him to go topside?"

"To vex him."

"Well say, Keyes, that's very good."

"If he got sore enough he'd stay in the bar."

"She told all this to the cops?"

"She's a thoroughbred, Ed."

"Just how do you figure she's bred so high?"

"She's covering scandal."

"Sperry's?"

"With—whoever."

"Oh, say it, I don't mind."

"His former wife, would be my guess."

"If so, why did she remind him?"

"Well, you can hardly blame her, another way you look at it, if she knew he did have a date with Mrs. Delavan, for not wanting a stood-up lady to come roaring down to the bar and letting the whole world in on it. If he had a date he had one, and there was nothing she could do about it. But at least she could make sure that the date was where it was supposed to be and not all over the hotel. She could localize it, as they say in medicine, and pretend she didn't care."

"So she called him?"

"Ed, she could hardly anticipate that—"

"Jane would up with his heels and heave him out the window?"

"Whatever she did."

"You ever pushed somebody out of a window?"

"No."

"O.K., try."

I stood up in front of the window and kept egging him on to try and push me out. He kept saying I was leaving out the big element

that had to be considered, which was surprise, and I kept saying if anybody could get
me out, with the sill across my waist, and
the sash across my eyes, they were probably
a wrestler but not likely a slim, small girl that
didn't weigh but 105 pounds. After a while
he got sore, and I piled in: "O.K. then,
Keyes. You've let a woman take you like
Grant took Richmond, but now you get it."

I told him about the dog, and all the things
Jane and I had figured out, and he had pink
from the winter nip when he came in there,
but now he got white, gray, and green.
There's a couch in there in the office where
I sometimes have a nap, and he went over
and lay down. "You think this is something
I just dreamed up? You think—?"

But he waved his hand for me to shut up
and I did. For a long time he lay there, as
sick a thing in the way of a man as I ever
hope to look at. Once he opened his eyes
and said: "Did Mrs. Delavan tell this to the
cops? I mean, about the dog?"

"She answered their questions. They
didn't ask her about any dog and she didn't
tell them. She stuck to what she knew. The
dog, if you want to make something of it,
that's in the realm of conjecture."

"Then that's all right."

It was along toward sundown of a winter Saturday when he finally stood up and went over to the window and stood staring out at the city. He looked like an old man. "Ed, I'm powerful hard hit."

"I'm sorry, Keyes."

"It goes together like a clock. Clears it all up."

"Not quite all. That maid—"

"Simple."

"Not to me. She didn't even like Mrs. Sperry. She—"

"The maid was not in on it."

"Even you thought she lied."

"Did you ever see the play Macbeth?"

"In college we played Macbeth. I was Banquo."

"Fine, then you'll understand what I see in this. In Macbeth, a man suspects that another man suspects him. Macbeth has an idea, from something peculiar about the murder of Duncan. So what does Macbeth do? Banquo has nothing on him. It's all in the realm of what Banquo thinks. So to get rid of Banquo he puts himself in the power of three thugs, who he hires to kill Banquo. Bad, Ed. A very bad play. But it brings out the principle involved here. Only a fool would put herself in the power of a Cockney servant girl on something like this, especially when she didn't need her help, or anybody's. Therefore we can only conclude she got in the girl's power by accident."

"Meaning?"

"Ed, she was up there. Jenkins was."

"And saw it?"

"Just happened to. And cashed in."

". . . What would she be doing there?"

"At that hour of night, I would say there was only one thing she would be doing, and that would be lolly-gagging with a guy. For a little slavey that sleeps in one of the small inside rooms down over the kitchen and isn't allowed to bring anybody in there, that just about would be the answer. She was up there, snugged into a canvas swing with a guy, and here comes this little procession of a man, a woman, and a dog. She keeps quiet, hoping not to be seen, and we can pretty well be sure that the guy, whoever he was, wanted it that way too. The procession marches around, and she sees it's Sperry, Mrs. Sperry—and who else does she see, Ed?"

"Dolly."

"Who can't talk, but can tell tales."

"But why that story Jenkins told the cops?"

"There was nothing else for her to do."

"What reason did she have?"

"To protect Mrs. Sperry, for a price, we can assume. To get it off the roof."

"And why Mrs. Sperry's story at the inquest?"

"The insurance investigators. If they could hang it on Mrs. Delavan, they'd save themselves every cent of their obligation. Therefore, they'd dig. But digging, real digging, was what Constance dare not have. If she hadn't been seen, then the plant that was made by the phone call, with the location of the body, would have made Mrs. Delavan guilty, so fine. But once there was evidence against *herself*, once there was stuff those insurance guys might turn up, she had to do something to get them out of the picture. On suicide, they were satisfied. So she made it suicide. She thought fast."

"Nice."

"Horrible."

We walked out to the street, and he took my arm. "Ed, I can be thankful of one thing, though."

"Yeah? What's that?"

"It's not my case."

"I guess that helps."

"But, Ed, suppose I had to pin it on her!"

He went back to Los Angeles, and for a couple of weeks all that happened was the itching I did over the $25,000 in insurance Jane had thrown away by firing Jenkins. But then one day Jane rang me and said the police wanted to talk to her again, and could I be there. This time it was a couple of plainclothes men, by the name of Brady and Lindstrom, and I think it was Lindstrom that did the talking. He fished a gold bracelet out of his pocket that was bent up quite a little and had three horses' heads on it with rubies for eyes. Or garnets, whatever they were. Nobody quite seemed to know. He asked Jane if she'd ever seen it before, and she said: "Yes, it's mine."

"Where'd you get this here bracelet?"

"From a cousin of mine."

"What's his name?"

"Harold Sherman."

"When was this?"

"About ten years ago. When I was in school. I rode three of his horses to firsts in a Long Island horse show, and this was his way of thanking me. I'm sure, if you'll look, you'll find some sort of engraving inside there about it."

"When did you wear it last?"

"I've never worn it."

"Why not?"

"Well, it's pretty ghastly, you know."

Lindstrom looked at it and Brady looked at it and they kind of looked at each other. You could tell that something being pretty ghastly was a new idea to them. So far as they knew, if it was gold and it had jewels in it, it must be O.K. and if she said she'd never worn it, it was a 2-1 shot she was lying. Lindstrom said: "Who has been wearing it?"

"Nobody that I know of."

"When did you miss it?"

"I haven't missed it."

"You didn't know it was gone?"

"Not until now."

". . . Where you been keeping it?"

"I haven't the faintest idea."

"What do you mean by that?"

"I mean I put it away when it was given me, I don't recall now just exactly where. I wrote a polite note about it, and forgot it. I haven't seen it since—I can't say when."

"You got a jewel box?"

"Yes, of course."

"Didn't you keep it there?"

"I tell you, I don't know. It could be."

"I'll have a look at this here jewel box."

I said: "No, you won't."

". . . Hey, Mac, who are you?"

"A friend. And my name's not Mac. It's Horner, like you were told. And the lady's not some tart in the Monday line-up. She's accommodated you so long as it was a question of clearing up a case that seemed to be giving you some trouble. Now it involves going into her jewel box that's different and how'd you like to get the hell out?"

"Mac, I don't care for that kind of talk."

"A judge'll be talking to you in an hour if—"

"O.K., O.K., if that's how you want it."

"Beat it."

It took me an hour to get her quiet again, but then I called a Lieutenant I knew over at headquarters to find out what it was about. It was a couple of hours before he called me back. "Ed, it was found on the street, the way I get it, the night Sperry took his dive. Found by a brother and sister on their way home from a bowling alley and they advertised it in the Register, under found, by the name of Jane and by the name that was engraved on it. They didn't get any answer so they advertised again. And then Lindstrom, he got interested in it, why Jane didn't come to get her bracelet so he went over there to talk to them. He traced who it belonged to by the New York jeweler that made it, and that's about all I can tell you, but I guess Lindstrom wanted to know more about it on account of that other stuff that's been turned up."

"O.K., thanks."

Jane and I figured on that a while, and after she said: "Ed, I'm getting frightened. It's more of that devilish plan. She threw that down there at the time she pushed him over."

"How would she have it?"

"I could have left it in Bermuda."

"Any way you can prove you did?"

"Jenkins might know. She packed me."

"If we could get out of her whether you brought it with you or left it in Jamaica that would be a help."

"I'll get her up here."

"She still here?"

"I suppose so.

I give you one guess, though, what the answer was on that. She had checked out without giving a forwarding address or anything. "All right, Ed, I'll say it since you won't. Firing her was just about the stupidest thing I ever did in my life, and you warned me, I can't say you didn't."

"We'll find her."

But suppose you try finding a Cockney girl that walked out the side door with her suitcase in her hand and just vanished. We hung around the gambling halls, the bus depots, the taxi stands; we called up all the little hotels. After three or four days I knew it was one for a detective, and we went to a guy on Fourth Street that we picked out of the classified phone book, though not anybody the company had ever done business with. He made a lot of notes, took my check for $150, explained there was quite a lot of preliminary expense getting out dodgers for his correspondents, that seemed to be people that kept an eye on cars and so on, and liked to pick up some dough on missing persons and didn't mind a little Hawkshaw excitement in their lives. But his face gave a twitch when we said we had no photograph, and I knew it was going to be tough.

About a week after that, when I went up one afternoon to take Jane out to dinner, I found her all in, hanging onto herself till her fingernails were cutting the palms of her hands to keep from breaking out into screaming hysteria. And come to find out the bishop's granddaughter was in town and had come to see her about Delavan. It seemed he didn't want to marry her any more, which might explain why Delavan was so nice about it when Jane started her period of residence all over again. "Ed, she was here for two hours—three hours, I don't know, I thought she'd never go. And what can I do for her? She's a frizzle-haired, washed-out pint-size simpleton. She talks baby talk. Even when she's trying to be sensible she talks it. And she's been perfectly horrible for Tom. For years and years she's been in his hair, and don't ask me what hold she was on him. He's known her ever since they were children, and God knows what went on. Nothing, probably. She wouldn't have enough gump for something really scandalous. But somehow, maybe because she's so tiny, maybe because she plays on his sympathies or something, that guilt complex of his gets into it, and he's alternately involved with her and trying to break away from her. That's all I was. He calls it rebound, but it was more than that. One more lunge at freedom for his soul. That he never gets. Now he's lunging again and she's after him again. Why don't they get married, and give the rest of the world some peace?"

"What did you tell her?"

144

"That I was sorry."

"Has she seen him?"

"He refuses to see her."

"And she wants you to intercede?"

"And I won't."

"Good."

". . . *Ed!*"

"Yeah?"

"Tom would know about the bracelet!"

"He might, at that."

"Well, she helped, after all!"

She went in the bedroom and talked, and came back looking better. "He says he's sure I haven't had any such thing since he met me, or he'd have known it. He reminded me that he inventoried everything just after the wedding, in connection with a new floater policy for the house, and he was very careful about everything of mine, especially my jewelry and coats, and he's positive, there was no such bracelet. And if there's any trouble about it, he's willing to testify, or talk to the police, or do whatever is necessary."

"You didn't actually ask him to go to the police?"

"No, I said if, as and when needed."

"O.K."

Couple of days later, I was over at a trucking

company's offices, trying to close a group deal. Stuff like that is mostly a matter of corporation taxes, and I was lining it out for a bunch of execs in the secretary's office, when a girl came in and said I was wanted on the telephone and that it was important. I took it outside, on her phone, and it was my secretary, Linda. "Mr. Horner, I've been trying to reach you all over town. Mr. Delavan's been killed."

"*What?*"

"They called us, on account of our card in his pocket."

"Who called?"

"The state police."

"The *state* police?"

"He fell from a horse. Outside of town."

"When was this?"

"They called twenty minutes ago and they're going to call again as soon as they get him back to town. What shall I tell them?"

"I'll take over."

Part Four:
Hush Money

Chapter Twelve

Taking over, that day anyway, consisted of sitting in Jane's living room and answering police questions over the telephone, mostly about who would claim the body, stuff like that. He'd been found in a gully after his horse, that he'd rented from the Los Amigos stables just south of town, had come in without him. For some of the stuff they wanted we had to call the family in the East, and Jane did the talking on that, and on breaking the news to this girl he'd been engaged to marry, Faith Converse. Jane called her Penny, but I think that was some moniker they'd given her, on account of her being so small. It took us until five, and they said as neither one of us was with him there'd be no need for us to attend the inquest, which would be held at another undertaking parlor that night. I suggested we drive over to Carson for dinner, and she seemed to like the idea. She had taken it a little hard for a couple of minutes, more from shock than anything else, I think, and then she had snapped out of it and done what she had to do in a quiet way I fell for pretty hard. But on a chance to get away from the hotel and the phone calls, she jumped at it pretty quick.

We had dinner in the Arlington, which was where we generally went over there, and we didn't talk about it, or ourselves, or anything of that kind. I got off on a long educational pep talk about Kit Carson, that the town was named after, and what a terrific help he'd been to all those old grizzlies that were building the West a hundred years ago. But on the way back we got to what was on our mind, and it was she that brought it up. "Ed, you know what this means, don't you?"

"That you don't need a divorce?"

"I've no further business in Reno."

"None at all?"

". . . That's for you to say."

"Then—O.K., you've got business."

"You want me to stay on?"

"Of course I do."

"We can't be married right away."

"You mean it wouldn't look right?"

"It's out of the question."

"Then you stay on, Jane, and we'll ride around and see each other and little by little two or three months will go by and a ceremony will be O.K."

"I'd say about six."

"Then six."

"Shall I write my family?"

"Go right ahead."

". . . Or perhaps I'll wait."

"Why wait, Jane? Write 'em."

"What's not announced doesn't have to be openly admitted. And what *is* announced can't be taken back. Just to avoid complications, I think I'm staying on for the climate. Or the scenery. Or something like that. You've got to admit it's pretty wonderful."

"Anything you say."

I tossed it off like a big shot that had it all under control, but inside me was something moving, like in the shark that swallowed the oyster borer. I had to tell her about that policy, and it would mean she'd know I'd lied to her, and big as the policy was, somehow I hated to get to it. But pretty soon I knew I had to, so I kept right on the big shot line and tossed it out like it was the big surprise good news I had been saving for her all the time. "And by the way, speaking of what's pretty wonderful, there's a wedding present due to drop in your lap, or a dowry, or whatever you call it, that's just about as wonderful as anything I can think of, anyway for a night in late fall."

"Dowry? What do you mean?"

"$100,000."

". . . For me?"

"For cute little you."

"From where?"

"That—policy."

". . . Tom's?"

"You didn't think I really knocked it in the head, did you?"

"But Ed, I haven't it."

"I have."

We rode quite some ways and she didn't say anything. Then: "Ed, I wish you hadn't done this to me."

"Made you $100,000, you mean?"

"Behind my back. Why *did* you?"

"Insurance is my life. I believe in it."

"I wish I could believe that was the only reason."

"That's one thing about dough, Jane. It'll do just as much for you whether you work for it or you don't work for it or whether you believe or you don't believe. It's strictly open shop. I'm not ashamed of it and I saw something good, something good for you I mean, and took it even when you told me not to."

"And you told me an untruth about it."

"Hell, I lied. But you'll get the money."

"And you'll get the cup."

". . . What cup?"

"Please, Ed."

"Can't a guy have *two* reasons for doing something?"

"Not if one of them's me."

We went along for a while trying to talk about what a pretty night it was, and how nothing ever looked as bright as lights in the clear Nevada air. Then she began to cry. "Ed, I've been trying to make myself say thank you for what you did. I suppose you had no bad motive. I can't do it. I—just can't."

"I can. I thank myself a lot."

"Then, all right."

"And not only for the money."

"I hope you enjoy the cup."

"And my wife."

"I—don't understand you."

"O.K., Jane, now you get it. I've never been quite sure, if you want to know the truth, about how Sperry got it. O.K., so the dog went over the wall. O.K., so you don't know a thing about the phone call. O.K., but there's the big Sperry policy, and unless they can prove suicide, there's the money. Now I know I lied to you about this Delavan policy. You couldn't have had anything to do with it. That clears up a lot of things. Maybe one's not got anything to do with the other, but it's got a lot to do with how I feel about it."

"Ed, *you* suspected me?"

"No, but it's nice being sure."

"Then you did suspect me?"

"I'd have loved you, anyhow."

"You could love me, suspecting—"

"I didn't care."

Brother, if I could leave it out about the next three hours I'd do it, and if that would be lying, I'd got to the point where one lie more or less didn't seem to matter a whole lot, one way or the other. But there's two or three people that could call it on me, so here goes, but don't get too excited about it if I kind of go easy and not take extra billboard space to advertise what a heel I felt like for a while. It'll be the truth but kind of on the quiet side, if you get what I mean—in good taste, but not any production job, with lights. We rode along, and she kept staring in front of her, and I kept trying to think of something like the Nevada air we could use for talk. We got to the hotel and started through the lobby and Lindstrom got up out of a chair and came over to us. Then he introduced a kid named Kubic that he said was assistant state's attorney. Then he asked Jane to sit down. She did and we all did and he asked if she was holding a policy on Delavan's life. "I don't, but I understand one was taken out for me."

"Who has this policy?"

"This gentleman here."

"What's he got to do with it?"

I said: "I'm the agent."

"And what are you doing with it?"

"Holding it for her benefit."

"Why you and not her?"

"I'm going to marry her."

It wasn't until the flicker. came in his eye that I realized how that sounded, and how it could even tie me in without in anyway including her out. "I see. I get it now, pal. And how much was this life insurance?"

"$100,000."

"You putting a claim in, Miss?"

"I don't know."

"You bet she's putting a claim in."

"O.K."

They left and we went on upstairs. When we got to her suite I said: "Well, it's easy to see whose fine Italian hand that is. Mr. Keyes has got into it again, as there's nobody here that knows about that policy."

But she started to tremble, and then she

began to cry, awful quivering sobs that nothing I did could stop. And she acted like I wasn't even there. There didn't seem much for me to do but go, so I did. But my three hours wasn't up yet.

It was after eleven when I got to the apartment house, but the operator goes off and the door locks at ten, so when I saw a woman sitting over by the lobby fireplace it meant she'd been waiting some little while. It wasn't till I heard my name called that I saw it was Mrs. Sperry. I said: "Well—this is an honor. To say nothing of a surprise."

"Mr. Horner, I have to talk to you."

We sat down and I helped her out of her coat. She had on house pajamas, some dark color, blue, I think, and I got a load of the figure. Then she began to talk. "I had a chat with Mr. Keyes today."

"I thought he was in Los Angeles."

"He called me from there. He's flying here."

"Tonight?"

"Tomorrow some time."

"I had supposed he would."

"On this Delavan case."

"He's hipped on the subject that Mrs. Delavan murdered her husband, Mrs.

Sperry, and he's probably hipped that she killed Delavan. If she ever murdered anybody, then we're all Chinamen."

"As I've tried to tell him."

"Oh, you've discussed it with him?"

"And I think annoyed him."

"He seemed to like you."

"Until recently."

"He gave you the air?"

"I haven't heard from him at all."

She looked at the fire some more, and said: "Mr. Horner, it would be a great deal better, for everybody concerned, if Mr. Keyes could be persuaded to let this thing rest. I don't know Mrs. Delavan, but she was briefly a part of my husband's life, and I don't relish even the sideswipe of scandal. It is in your power to have Mr. Keyes taken off this case?"

"It is not."

"Can't you suggest it?"

"I can and I will."

"It won't help?"

"Not if he really tears in."

"What is his interest in it?"

"A $100,000 insurance risk that my company is on."

"And that's all?"

"How do you mean, that's all?"

"If that were paid, would his interest cease?"

". . . Are you willing to pay it?"

"Possibly you don't know. I have some means."

"I heard you were rich."

"I—have some means."

I told her it was the kind of stuff that insurance companies don't like and have to watch close any time they have to fool with it, or think they have. I explained how it was all tied up with concealment of evidence of a crime, and while often a go-between is used on the recovery of stolen jewels, the company is pretty safe as it can always say the stuff they paid a reward for was represented to them as found, not stolen. "On a case like this, it would have to be done through the beneficiary. If she would accept indemnity from somebody else, I think you would have to leave the company out of the deal and she would have to renounce claim by admission of some misrepresentations in connection with the application, or something of that sort, and even that would be pretty hard because she wasn't the one that applied."

"But it could be worked out?"

"I'm not sure."

"But it might be?"

"I don't say it couldn't."

"Mr. Horner."

"Yes?"

"Will you be my go-between?"

Now, believe it or not, what was running through my mind, even after all that Jane had figured out on her, was that it didn't seem possible she could be guilty of anything, and so far as being willing to pay $100,000 to hush it up went, that might look funny in somebody else, but for a woman that had $20,000,000 how funny was it? But by now, she was leaning toward me, where I was sitting beside her on the sofa, in a queer, please-please, way, and then I felt something shoot through me. Because, from the look in her eye, I knew if I wanted to take her upstairs, there was nothing she'd stop at to get me to be her go-between. Then, for the first time I knew, without there being any question about it, she was guilty, not only of Sperry's death, but of Delavan's.

I took her hand and gave it a little pat, and she took mine and gave it a squeeze, and smiled again. I said: "I'm sorry; but I wouldn't touch it, or anything connected with it, with a ten-foot pole."

Her face almost seemed to fall apart, and

after a while she licked her lips on the inside, the way people do to keep them from twitching. She said: "But—but—what am I going to do?"

"Get ready to take it, I guess."

"*Take it!* . . . What do you mean?"

"Scandal. Isn't that what you said?"

"Oh . . . Yes, that's what I said."

"Unless you've forgotten."

She got up, went clumping over to the door like she had lost the use of her legs. I let her out. Then I phoned Jane. I phoned her three times, and each time she hung up on me. The fourth time the hotel operator said the orders were she was not to be disturbed.

Chapter Thirteen

The wire from Keyes was waiting for me at the office next morning, and around eleven I drove over and met him at the airport. With him was Norton. Not much was said going over to the office, but as soon as we got there, Keyes said: "Mr. Norton, I think you'd better tell Ed what we agreed on coming up."

"Ed, I have bad news for you."

"O.K., so I'm fired."

"Wait now, not so fast."

"My heart's not broke as I told you before."

"Temporarily relieved, if you'll let me talk."

"About the same, isn't it?"

"No, it's not. Keyes has insisted on it, not because he thinks you made a mistake in insisting on this policy, and in fact making an issue of it, as you recall you did, for he thinks anybody has the right to make a mistake, and everybody ought to make an issue of what he regards as a matter of principle. It's not that. But he does feel that you're bound up with too close a personal tie to the person most involved in this to be disinterested and helpful agent. But if our investigation shows the person most involved is not involved at all, believe me, Ed, you'll be reinstated, and I'm sure Keyes joins me in the wish that that's the way it's going to turn out."

"Absolutely."

"Well, the same to you, Keyes, and many of them."

"Thanks, Ed, thanks."

"What for?"

"Well—it sounded friendly."

"Not if you were listening it wasn't. And

especially if you were listening to J. P. here, and what he said about the person most involved. You stupid jerk, don't you know who did this?"

"I think so."

"I don't think. I know. It was La Sperry."

"That's ridiculous."

"She was around last night."

". . . Around where?"

"To see me. To get you called off."

"I don't believe you."

"To buy you off."

"Now Ed, I know it's a lie."

"To buy General Pan Pacific off. To pay that claim."

"What are you trying to tell me?"

"Keyes, how would I know you called her last night from Los Angeles if she didn't tell me? You called her and told her you were coming. All of a sudden you thought this proved that all that stuff about the dog didn't mean anything in connection with the death of Sperry, and you couldn't wait to call her up to say 'here I come.' You did, didn't you? And it was the first call you've made in some time, wasn't it? O.K., she's scared worse of you than you ever were of her, or anything. So the same to you and many of them, but just how disinterested and helpful you're going to be I wouldn't like to say—not in the presence of witnesses."

"Ed, on this subject you're getting unbalanced."

Norton kept looking at me, like he was trying to dope the thing out, and then he reached for the telephone. I had forgotten he knew Mrs. Sperry, but in a few seconds he was talking to her like they used to be pals and then he banged her right between the eyes with it, the offer she had made me the night before. She held him on the line I guess twenty minutes and he talked pleasant and friendly the one or two things he said, but mostly it was "I see," "I see," and some more "I see." When he hung up he said; "It sounds awfully funny that a woman would be willing to kick in $100,000 to hush something up, until you recall how much money Constance Sperry has, and what an awful mess it's going to mean if we do go ahead on this, especially as the papers will unquestionably do everything they can to drag her in, even if it's only indirectly, as that would blow the story up big."

"Then why don't you take her up?"

"Ed, first let's let Keyes do his stuff."

"Yeah, but will he?"

"Well, Keyes, what about it?"

163

"Put somebody else on it if you want."

I said: "If you've got any sense you *will* put somebody else on it, and put us *both* on suspension. I'm telling you, La Sperry killed Delavan, as she killed her husband. She killed her husband so she could marry some X guy not identified yet, and I don't think it's Keyes. She killed her husband after an annulment idea fell through and as he wouldn't give her a divorce she had to use a little direct action, or thought she did. What she killed Delavan for I don't know, and how she killed him I don't know, but if you'd only hold everything a day or two until I locate an English maid that seems to know more than she's told, I think I can fill in whatever it is we don't know. I've got detectives trying to find her, and I don't think they'll be so long."

Keyes had listened to this with a face like it was cut out of stone, and what he felt about it he didn't say. But he had Norton over a barrel, because back of it all was the fact that Keyes had been trying to block this policy, and there wasn't much Norton could do now but let him have his way. He thought quite a while, and went out in the ante-room and sat in the spare chair and in a minute Linda came in with me and Keyes to leave

164

him alone. Then after a while he was back. "All right, Keyes, take over. Ed, I'll walk home with you."

We went out and started down the street and in a different tone of voice asked me for the lowdown on Mrs. Sperry, and why I was so sure she had done it. I said; "There's no low-down, nothing I could prove in court, just something she pulled when she was talking to me last night, kind of a pass she made at me, that only a desperate woman would make, and I'll be damned if I believe people get that desperate over something like scandal. If that was all, couldn't she leave town? She's got the dough to go to Siam, if she wants to. Keyes, he's awfully proud of himself that he knows, most of the time, without knowing how he knows. O.K., that's how I know now."

"That, I confess, shakes me."

"However, we've got other things to talk about. I still have that policy.

"Our policy? On Delavan?"

"That's it."

We walked on, as far as my apartment, and went up there, and I talked and kept on talking. I told him what had happened on the policy, just as I've told it here, but on certain points I told them over two or three times

so there couldn't be any question I was trying to make myself look good. I told it like
it was, and he didn't often interrupt. Then
I said: "But that's not all. I mailed it to
myself, but I won't tell you to what address, and I won't tell you where it is now.
Until this thing happened, Delavan's death,
I mean, it was a question of something I
wanted, the company cup; something I
thought was good for her, the protection that
I meant to get for her even if she was acting
silly about it; and Keyes's nonsense, that got
under my skin, and plenty. But it's moved
past any of that. It's a question of her—Jane
Delavan, I mean, and cops and charges and
things I can't even anticipate. It just so hap-
pens she prefers not to see me at the moment, and maybe never will again. But on
how I feel about it, if it costs me my job,
if it costs you $100,000 or $1,000,000, or
it costs Keyes his mind, if he's got one—I
put her ahead of any of that and all of that.
And you might as well know it. I think if anything is done about that policy now, it could
boomerang on her—I mean if I took it somewhere, if I turned it in on you, if I sent it
to her, if I joggled it in any way. I'm sorry.
The company's been swell to me and you
have and allowing I don't think he's all there

in the head, Keyes has. But on this, I'm rock."

He took a minute or two after I stopped, and I'm proud to set it down here, word for word as well as I remember it, and I think it's engraved in my mind pretty good, what he said, which was: "I can see, Ed, why you attach importance to this, and in fact seem to be pretty well rung up about it. However, there are two questions in connection with it, and I think you've got them pretty thoroughly confused. The first one is: What should you have done, after you and Keyes came in from the mountains and he had given you his dress rehearsal of the moving finger's drama—when you heard what the cop said about the death at the hotel, and were faced with a decision as to what should be done, about the policy and Delavan's check. I don't in any way follow you as to the horrendous nature of your decision. If you had got Delavan's check back from the post office certainly you would have held onto the policy pending more details on the death, and just as certainly when you found it was not Delavan who was killed, as Keyes thought, but Sperry, you would have sent the check on again, without Delavan's being any the wiser, and the result wouldn't have been in any way different. For my part, when I was crying to work the thing out I think if there was any doubt in my mind I would have held things up. But on the basis of things as they stood then, I'm not at all sure that I wouldn't have done just what you did, considering I had given you a green light, as I did, and considering how little importance was to be attached to Keyes. at the moment, moving-finger previews or not, on account of his imbecile infatuation with Constance Sperry, and the silly monkeyshines he was indulging in on account of it. That, I think, takes care of the first question.

"The next question is what you should do about the policy now. You seem to have some idea I expect you to turn it over to me, apparently under the impression that now Delavan's dead, and the beneficiary has never had the policy, I can escape liability, or that no claim can be made, or whatever it is that's in your mind. In the first place, when we took Delavan's money, the policy's in force, and we're liable. In the second place, if I attempted to avoid liability, it would cost me more than I could possibly gain. It would cost me you, for one thing. Let me do that and you can't sell for General Pan, that I'll promise you. You're an idealist, a fanatic, on insurance in general and this company in particular. But let this happen and you'll have to move to another company, as you've once or twice told me you might do—simply because as a fanatical idealist you wouldn't believe in this company any more. In the third place, you can rest quite assured that if any fact disclosed by the investigation relieves me of liability, on a suicide clause, complicity of the beneficiary in homicide, as Keyes insists may be the case, or anything else, I am going to deny liability and refuse to pay until a court compels me. I may wish I didn't have to, but I have stockholders to think of, and don't you get the idea I'll be soft-hearted in any way. I'll be tough, down to the last comma of the bond. In the final place, however, which is the main place, so far as I'm concerned—are you listening, Ed?"

"I am, J. P."

"I pay what I owe, period, new paragraph."

His face tightened, as he said that, and I knew that maybe paying what he owed had cost him something now and then, but as I say, I felt proud of him. I didn't feel much better about most of it, because we were talking about terrible things, at least as far as Jane was concerned. But at least I knew I could still call my friend one man that meant something to me. We sat there a few minutes, and he said:

"I'd like you to know, Ed, I had to humor Keyes after his efforts to block that policy, which of course would have saved us the rap, if we'd listened to him. But I came here prepared to pay on the nail, as I've told you I make a practice of doing. He doesn't know it, but there's a cashier's check for $100,000 in my pocket right now, made out to Jane Delavan. I have it with me."

"That doesn't surprise me."

"I wanted you to know."

"That pleases me."

I ate lunch somewhere, maybe the Bonanza. It seemed funny not to be with Jane, and pretty soon I called her. A woman answered. She said Jane wasn't in. I asked who she was and she said she was taking all Mrs. Delavan's calls. It turned out later she was a nurse that had been called in on account of a crackup Jane had had, but it hit me in the stomach to be given a brush-off. I left word I had called and went on out to the Scout Ranch, changed into riding clothes, and went on back for the Count. At least

I could exercise him, now the situation had changed but there was no way to tell him so. I found him out back, tied up to a post, with Jackie wiping him off. She said hello and to get Red, one of their trail horses, out of the first stable, or she'd do it for me if I could wait a minute. I said: "Well, thanks, he's O.K., but I've got one of my own or have I?"

"You mean—him?"

"I do—unless we've all gone crazy."

"Well maybe we have—or one of us, anyway."

She stared at me, and certainly looked like she thought I was slightly off my nut at least. Then she said; "He's had his workout—all he wants for one day."

"You mean you worked him?"

"Who do you think worked him?"

My heart gave a jump. There was no reason why Jackie should know about the mess things were in, or what was in the envelope she had, or anything that would cause her to fit two and two together. It did something for me, to know Jane had been there, and really was out when I called, and had worked the Count, even if she was busted up with me. But after a while, riding Red up in the hills, I slipped down again, my morale, I mean. She wouldn't let the Count down, whatever happened, or any animal that needed her, so what it proved about me was practically nothing.

When I got in Jackie propositioned me about buying Red and using him. I asked why. "Well, that horse of yours is coming around so pretty, on manners and all, he's practically a sure bet for five gaits in any show from San Diego on up the coast, and it sure seems a shame for you to begin all over again, and ruin him. Red's a nice horse. You could do with him."

"I'll think about it."

It left me kind of wilted. As property, the Count was mine whenever I claimed him. As horse, he had passed over, and didn't belong to me any more.

Around 9:30 the outside phone rang in my apartment and it was Norton, wanting to know if he could come over. I said come on and put out highball makings but when he got there he didn't want a drink. He said: "Keyes has found that maid."

"Just for curiosity, how? I couldn't?"

"Gas turn-on."

"Gas—?"

"The turn-on slip, on her gas. He figured

your detective had probably covered rooming houses, filling stations, hotels, bus depots, and other places people leave tracks when they think they fade out. When there was no sign of her he concluded she was really dug in, in a hideout somewhere, so she wouldn't run into people. That meant a house, an apartment, or something like that. But one thing she'd have to have would be gas. So, as they only get four or five new applications a day at this little company here, it was duck soup for him. She was using a phony name but the turn-on clerk remembered her right away by the Cockney accent."

"Simple, but I never thought of it."

"I never thought of it either, but if it was a needle in a haystack he'd have some simple magnet sent over and five minutes later Mr. Needle would be hanging to it. You heard of Faith Converse?"

"Delavan's ex-fiancee?"

"She's in it now."

"How?"

"Possible murderess, accomplice, or both."

"Boy, oh boy, J. P., is that one on Keyes?"

"It's thrown Keyes back on his heels, but good, because of course if she did this

Delavan job we pay. But I don't mind telling you Keyes is under my skin a little just now, and any little thing that gave him his come-uppance would come under the head of good news, even if it did cost us $100,000."

"Yeah, but say something. About this Converse."

"Delavan gave her the air."

"That's what brought her here."

"Keyes found out all about that as soon as he got Delavan's family on the telephone, to see what they knew, or maybe thought. They knew a little and they thought plenty, and most of it centered on this girl—"

"Known also as Penny."

"That's it. So he's been trying to get in touch with her. But after he called the gas company about the turn-on slips, and I helped out with some comsha so the little turn-on girl would forget the rules and let him have a look, he stepped over to the police department to see the reports on the sale of firearms. The stores turn them in, and he's found that generally, on a real hideout, the party of the first part likes a gun around the house, just in case. So he didn't find anything that looked like it might be Harriet Jenkins in blackface, but he did find Faith Converse."

"*She* bought a gun?"

"A nice little .38 automatic."

"What do you make of it?"

"Nothing, but I wish I'd never heard of Thomas Delavan.

"That I can understand."

He began walking up and down my apartment, poured himself a spoonful of Scotch, walked up and down some more. The phone rang. I answered, and my heart skipped a beat when I heard the same old Cockney voice drop the H off my name. "Yes, Jenkins, what is it?"

"I'd call a doctor if I was you, sir, accant Mr. Keyes. 'E acts very ill. 'E acts seriously ill, sir."

"What's happened?"

"Nothing, sir, but 'e's not 'imself."

"Where are you?"

"At 'is office, sir."

"You mean my office?"

" 'E said 'is office."

"I'll be over."

Norton was there beside me, close enough to hear all of it. I hung up and started to call a doctor, but he stopped me. "Let's see what it is, first." That made sense, and in about two seconds flat we had on our hats and coats and were on our way over there.

Chapter Fourteen

It was Jenkins, all right, but I don't think her own mother would have known her. Instead of the bombazine uniform and run-over shoes she used to wear she had on a mink coat, a good-looking black dress, green shoes, green alligator bag, and green hat, and her face was washed and had nice makeup on it, and even her hands were clean. I've told you about the shape. Now, for the first time, she looked like a really pretty girl, and about five years younger than I had taken her for. She was in the ante-room, where Linda sits, when we got there, but she took us back in the private office, where Keyes was stretched out on the couch, with his coat off and only the desk light lit. But he said he didn't want any doctor, and would be all right if we'd just let him alone a few minutes. We went out in the ante-room again and I closed the private office door and asked Jenkins what went on.

"As I told you, sir, nothing."

"What are you doing here?"

" 'E brought me 'ere."

"What for?"

"To tell what I knew about the death of Mr. Delavan."

"So you do know something about it?"

"Indeed I do, sir."

Norton began questioning her, and pretty soon she got pretty gabby. "It was around seven, I should say, when Mr. Keyes came to the little 'ouse I had rented on the edge of town, and I'd noticed 'im at the inquest over Mr. Richard, but 'adn't known 'im and supposed 'im an officer. Then 'e said 'oo 'e was, and when 'e said 'e was interested to go into the exact manner of Mr. Delavan's death, accant 'e was suspicious of it, I was quite willing to speak about it, as I'd about made up my mind already I was going to end my silence and tell what I knew. So 'e remained outside in a respectful and gentlemanly way while I dressed, brought me 'ere in the cab 'e had waiting, then took me to the room inside there and asked me a few questions, not many. Then in a most friendly and understanding way 'e said 'e never 'eckled a willing witness, and why didn't I sit down to the recording machine and tell my story on the record while 'e went out and had some coffee. So I did, only taking five records to do it as I made it very brief and clear. Then 'e came back and put the records on the machine and listened to what I 'ad said. And then 'e began looking bad. I did what I could. I got 'im water and 'elped 'im to the couch so 'e could lie down and then I rang you. I think it 'ad something to do with what e' was 'earing, if I may say what I think."

"Please do."

"Yes, feel perfectly free."

She sat down in Linda's chair and told it all over again, then noticed Norton doing some more marching around and offered him her place and he took it. He said afterwards he didn't often accept a seat from a lady, but she seemed to have the kind of legs that made it advisable she got perpendicular for a while. Keyes came out and she asked if she'd be needed any more that night. He said she would. The four of us went in the private office and he switched on the dictation machine.

The first of it was a lot of stuff about how lousy Mrs. Sperry had treated her in Bermuda, and she wasn't quite as brief and clear as she seemed to think. Then there was some stuff about how Jane had taken pity on, her and brought her here, 'aht of the goodness of 'er 'eart, and the trouble over the annulment. Then she told about how Delavan took her to court to put her under bail, and then here it began coming, the part that Jane and I could never figure out. It was all full of *ahts* and *hins* and *hopens* and *shahts* and *'earts* and *flahs*, and Linda didn't do anything about them, but anyway, here it is, the way it was transcribed with pothooks from the records early the next morning. Anyway, if it's not what she said it's what she thought she was saying:

"I was quite frightened in court, until I saw Mr. Delavan looking at me, and I knew he liked me, as I certainly did him. So a day or so later I thought I would see if I could play a little trick on him. So I went to a shop and called him by phone and asked him if I couldn't pay him a visit and talk to him about it. And as I expected, he said: 'Good God, girl, no. If this place is watched it would ruin me. I'd be forever blocked from bringing suit myself, and she could have anything she asked in court.'

" 'Then,' I said, 'why not visit *me?*'

" 'That would be worse,' he said.

" 'Perhaps not. If a young man came up on the Washoe-Truckee roof tonight, just to take the air, and he happened to find a young lady there with the same idea in mind, who would criticize him? It's a fine, open, respectable place so far as the law is concerned, and it has the additional advantage that it's quite deserted from ten o'clock on.'

" 'I couldn't dare risk it.'

" 'Wouldn't you like to risk it, though?'

" 'Shut up, limey, shut up.'

" 'Ah, come on.'

" 'No.'

"But I went up there, just the same, thinking he might change his mind. I waited a long time, in one of the big rocking sets with canvas sides and back, and he didn't come. But as I had just come to the conclusion I would be disappointed, the iron door that leads below slowly opened, and there he was, at first paying no attention to me, but walking cautiously around to make sure nobody else was there. Then he came over beside me, and I told him if he compelled me to be his witness, I would of course tell the truth about Mr. Sperry, that there had been no infidelity on his part with me, but I would also tell the truth about this night on the roof, that there had been infidelity on his own part to his own wife with me. And he looked at me sharply and asked what I meant by inventing such a falsehood. And I looked at him just as sharply, as I hope, and asked him what he meant by inventing such a false-hood himself, for he perfectly well knew he had overpowered me and torn off my clothes and used the badminton shuttlecock for a gag and worked his wicked will on me. And as I spoke I tore my dress and scratched my arm with one fingernail and showed him the badminton shuttlecock which I had in the pocket of my apron and had wet some time before at the hose tap in the corner. 'It is the truth, and you know it, my young and handsome friend,' I told him, 'and if you don't admit it I shall go right over to the phone there and call the hotel staff and you won't be able to get away before they nab you and my cuts and bruises will substan-tiate my tale. My very shocking tale, I may say.'

" 'But you're not offended?'

" 'Not if you let off my bail.'

" 'Then perhaps you enjoyed this frightful outrage?'

" 'Aren't you the roguish one.'

" 'And perhaps an encore is in order?'

"So he took me in his arms, and gave up the idea of annulment, though he didn't tell Mrs. Delavan at once, and when he did tell her, pretended Mr. Sperry had frightened him, as she had told him would happen, for we didn't want it known, the relationship that had sprung up between us. And repeatedly he said how happy he was, and how at least I had set him free from this frightful thing in his life, this woman in the east who he had married one girl to be free from, without success, but now, because he loved me, he felt the shackles had fallen from his heart. And I was happy too, and heard without sorrow the difficulty we would have over money, and how if he married against his family's wishes he would lose even the small income that he now had. For I took that to be his way of saying he might not be able to be married, on account of our different stations in life, and I didn't mind, because I loved him.

"And then one night as we sat there, the iron door opened and Mr. Sperry appeared with the little dog he loved so, and took with him wherever he went. I hadn't seen him in some time, and didn't know he was in Reno. Mr. Delavan and I kept perfectly still, and when Mr. Sperry went down after a few turns with the dog, we laughed with much enjoyment at how we had stayed hidden. Next night it was the same, except *she* was with him, Mrs. Sperry, and again we kept still, though wanting to laugh. Then, in a few minutes, she sat down on the wall, and he stood nearby smoking his pipe, several times warning her to be careful. Then she said oh damn, and told him her bracelet had fallen and was probably ruined, even if some passer-by happened to pick it up. Then soon she said: 'No, it didn't fall, either. Look, it's caught on the brace.'

"Then he looked and said that was indeed remarkable and she leaned out and tried to reach it, he at once catching her and pulling her back. 'Here,' he said, 'you hold the dog.' He had the dog in his arms, as he often did, and gave it to her. Then he lay down on the wall, holding onto it with one hand and reaching down with the other toward the steel truss that ins over to the neon sign over the street. She still held the dog, but stepped over behind him. Then she stooped quickly, and lifted his foot. Then he wasn't there any more. Then Mr. Delavan had his hand over my mouth to stifle my scream, and the little dog was moaning and she was standing there with her face raised to the sky. 'Thank God,' she said, 'thank the merciful God! It was an accident, you barely touched him, you can sleep this night—but he's gone. Get down to your room and wait for their call! If you go insane, wait for it!'

"And in a jiffy she was gone. 'And we can thank the merciful God too,' said Mr. Delavan, 'that we weren't seen, and won't be dragged in. It was a shocking thing, but there's nothing we can do for him now. You get down, too. Get down there and turn down the bed in my wife's room, or something, whatever you do at this hour. And be sure you ring about something on the phone, so you can prove you were there.'

" 'And where will you go?' I asked him.

" 'I'll think of some place.'

" 'Use the stairs,' I said."

She told how they raced down the stairs to the eleventh floor, she going to Jane's suite to see if Jane was still out, he to the stairs to slip on down and out through the basement without being seen. When she got to the suite she checked that Jane was still out, then called the operator to ask the time and tell her a little joke, she didn't say what, so the girl would remember the call. He went to some club, she didn't say which, and pledged his watch for some gambling dough, so the slip would show the date and the cashier would remember the time. Then he came to call on Jane. It was three o'clock in the morning, and Jenkins was in her own bed almost asleep when the grand scheme occurred to her. She got out of bed at once, went to a gambling hall, and called Delavan. There was no answer, and she went and threw gravel against the window of his room to wake him. Mrs. Sperry, she told him, when he let her in, could pay. At first he was against it, but the more she talked to him about how rich Mrs. Sperry was, and how they could hit her first for $100,000, then keep it up and keep it up, the more he weakened. They went in another gambling joint, rang her awake, and told her they were coming up. So they did, he going into the hotel the way he left it, she going up, in her uniform, in the regular elevator, as though she'd had a late call. She went on:

"She was quite nasty, but changed her melody when she saw we meant what we said. But she said it was out of the question the police should discover he had fallen from the roof. If they ever guessed she was up there, she felt they might guess the truth, so it was agreed that since Mrs. Delavan was out at the time, I could safely place Mr. Sperry in the suite. Little did I know, at that time, that she had contrived the whole thing, the exact spot on the wall and all, and if I may express my own opinion, had placed the bracelet where it seemed to have fallen, since it turned out to be Mrs. Delavan's bracelet, all in the way it occurred, with a telephone call and all the rest of it, to implicate Mrs. Delavan and save herself. This we learned much later, when Mrs. Delavan phoned Mr. Delavan about the bracelet and told him of the other things the police were pressing her about. This was when Mr. Delavan and I knew we had to tell what we knew at last, whether it meant losing our advantage or not."

There was a lot in there about getting the little house, and her keeping under cover in Reno, but going to Tonopah and Carson and Truckee in the new clothes Delavan bought her with the first money Mrs. Sperry let them have. The big dough she had to get from New York, by selling securities there, but she kicked in with $10,000 quick. Then at the inquest, Lynch spotted the insurance investigators, and she got scared to death. She thought the cops were the only ones she had to fool, but with an insurance company in, trying to hang it on the very one, Jane, that she had done her best to frame, she could see it coming they might find out the truth. That was when she got up at the inquest and told of seeing him jump. Then, Jenkins said:

"She pleaded with us, when we told her we were clearing up the suspicion she had created against Mrs. Delavan. We were not to be shaken, but we agreed at last, if she paid the $100,000, to say Mr. Sperry was on the roof alone with the dog, that he jumped, so it would correspond with her story, except she could say she had seen it in the dark and thought it was a window, and we could say we had withheld our evidence to keep out of trouble and to save his name from disgrace, as we regarded suicide as a scandalous thing. But then she said she would pay the $100,000 in cash, but as naturally so large a withdrawal would arouse interest at the bank, she didn't want to be seen talking with Mr. Delavan. Would he get a horse from one of the stables and ride over to the spot she described and meet her there? She was most insistent about it, and as the amount was so large and we needed it so badly, he finally agreed and I, fool that I was, let him go."

Her voice got a rasp to it then, and I saw Keyes brace himself. She went on: "And I swear as I sit here that she enticed him to this lonely spot to kill him, and that she did kill him, for with him out of the way it would be my word against hers, and I had already compromised my reputation for honesty by withholding my true story and telling a false one, at the inquest. I have been in hiding since Mrs. Delavan discharged me, but she had her very good reason and always treated me well, and I cannot remain silent, now I know how the affair stands."

That seemed to be all, and I switched off the machine and for a while we sat there, nobody looking at anybody else. Then Keyes held up one finger for us to hold everything, got up, and reached way over, to the doorknob, and jerked it open. Mrs. Sperry was there in the ante-room, leaning close to the door jamb to hear what went on inside. She came in and looked us over and then went over and held her face up to Keyes with tears running down. "You wouldn't believe anything this cheap little slut might say about me, would you?"

"Yes. I would and I do."

Chapter Fifteen

She sat down at my desk, and began to hook it up big on the weep stuff. Then she began begging Norton to pay no attention to anything Jenkins had told us, and kept saying to forget the insurance claim, that she'd pay it herself, that she was really thinking of Jane, because of course Jenkins had only cooked up this tale to shield her and eventually the truth would come out. Norton didn't even look at her, and it was when she went over and dropped on her knees beside him, and took his face in her hands to turn it toward her that we all jumped. Norton said later he knew at last how a man feels when he's out in a cemetery at night and a ghost comes floating up to him. How she got in we never found out, because while the street door was unlocked it seemed impossible we wouldn't have noticed somebody open it, and when she got in we never found out either, but stalking into the room, one step at a time, her eyes focused on Mrs. Sperry like somebody in a trance, and a horrible little grin on her face, was a tiny, pale, queer-looking woman, maybe thirty-five or so, in a black suit with black stockings, black shoes and a black hat. When she began to talk it was in a little high, squeaky, sing-song voice that sounded like some kid reciting stuff in Sunday School. She kept going closer to Mrs. Sperry, one step at a time, and as she moved she talked:

"It may help with him, going down on your knees, but it'll do you no good with me. You got away from me yesterday, but not this time, not tonight. Oh, I knew it was another woman, in spite of the lies he told me, but he wouldn't say who it was, and it wasn't till I followed him yesterday, in the car I rented, and saw him get on the bus, then get off at the riding stable, and come out in boots, and keep looking at his watch before they brought him the horse, that I knew he was meeting somebody. And I got out, and walked over the hill where I could see the whole bridle path, and there you were, with the golf bag over your shoulder, waiting, and at last I knew what you looked like. Then here he came, and you ducked behind the pinon tree until he had passed and turned off the path into the wash. Then you went after him, running. And I went after you. And when I reached the place you both turned off, where I could see, you were down on your knees to him too, and I was glad, whatever it was he had done to you, that you were paid in suffering for the suffering you had brought to me. Then you both started back, and he mounted. Then you dropped the scarf and he dismounted again to climb down into the gully and pick it up for you.

Then you swung the golf driver on his head and ran, and I was cheated, for I was waiting to kill you both, and all that came my way was the horse you slapped and started for home before you went running off toward the golf links. You escaped me then, and it wasn't until tonight, when you went hurrying out of the hotel that I got on your trail again, and could finally track you down. You'll not escape me now—"

Keyes grabbed her handbag and Norton grabbed her. She screamed but Norton held onto her while Keyes took the gun out of the bag and dropped it in a desk drawer. I called the cops.

In a couple of minutes a patrol car stopped outside and a couple of uniformed men came in. They began working on the little woman, who was Faith Converse, to make her stop screaming and kicking, and the way they did it was take off her shoes. After a couple of stomps in her stockinged feet she quit and began to cry. Then Lindstrom came in and began taking names. Then he listened to the records and while the uniformed cops were still working on Faith to get her in some kind of shape, he listened while I gave it to him what had happened in the gully. He nodded, pretty friendly. "We had it doped out something like that. We didn't know who yet, but we had a 100 per cent check on the wife all that afternoon. It wasn't her, we knew that. But we'd have had it."

All this time Keyes was sprawled on the sofa, staring at Mrs. Sperry like somebody sitting up with a corpse. Then he jumped, but he was too late. The report went off like a cannon shot in that enclosed space, but I'm afraid La Sperry didn't hear it. The .38 that Keyes had dropped in the desk drawer was right under her hand, where she was sitting, and she made an A-1 clean job of it.

By the time the police photographers got through, and Linda got there, and transcribed the Jenkins stuff for the reporters, and they took the body out, and a few other little things had been cleaned up, it was well after daylight, and I was out on my feet, and didn't get up until around four that afternoon. Around five, when I was dressed, there came a couple on the buzzer, and my heart jumped. I opened the door and it was Jane, in her gambling pants, with the mink coat on and the red ribbon around her hair.

I was so happy I couldn't talk for a minute, even after she was in my arms. "Mr. Horner, I hear you've a check for me."

"Somebody tell you that?"

"A certain Mr. Norton."

"Yes, the agent likes to deliver it in person. He gave it to me. However, I must say I'm surprised he looked you up."

"He wanted to meet the future Mrs. Horner."

"Shows he's got manners.

She cut out the gagging, then, looked me in the eye, and said: "Ed, when I got it all straight, from what he told me, that at last I've come to the end of it, these things that have dogged me the last three years, I could have kissed him. But I thought I'd come over and kiss you."

"Then let's begin."

"I looked after your horse, by the way."

"I know."

After a while we got around to the newspapers that she had with her, and looked at all our pictures, even my picture, that were smeared all over them, and read the story, and then we thought we better go over to the hotel and see how Keyes was making out. He was sitting not far from the porter's desk, where Norton was getting their transportation back to Los Angeles, and if he wasn't exactly what you'd call cheery and chipper, he was anyway quite a lot better. And while he started a long explanation to Jane of why he had pulled what he did, I drifted over to Norton and he gave me the recent developments. It seems there was a bill-fold, an alligator bill-fold, with a coronet burned on it, and initials, that had been turned in at the desk and that he'd been asked about, and it pretty well proved there was a lord or an earl or something who had been staying in San Francisco and visiting La Sperry week-ends. But instead of making Keyes sore, when he got it through his head at last what she'd been up to all the time, it relieved his mind. "Because," he told Norton, "if she'd rather choose the deep end than come to him with a stain on her escutcheon, that proves what I knew all the time, that she was a thoroughbred."

"Kind of a five-gaited job," I said to Norton.

"Or anyway five-faced, we could safely say."

So while we were snickering at that, they came over, Keyes looking very noble, Jane patting his hand in a forgiving kind of way.

And then Norton snapped his fingers and cocked his eye across the lobby and we all looked. And headed for the dining room, a $40 plumed hat on her head, $40 suede shoes on her feet, a $150 black crepe dress giving the works to her shape, and the mink coat hanging carelessly off her shoulders, was Jenkins, and a little bit behind her, but not too much behind her, a carnation in his buttonhole and a Swede grin on his face, was Lindstrom, the detective. We all wondered the same thing, whether this was some more police stuff that would mean we could begin to worry all over again, and it didn't take any high sign from Norton to start us all over to the dining room door. But by the time we got there we knew we could quit worrying. The captain was seating them, and he couldn't see it, but we could: Lindstrom was playing footie with her, and she was giving it the old Limehouse leer.

So that's how Jenkins came to live in Reno too, and how Jane, whenever she's got a big party coming on, has just about the slickest personal maid service anybody ever had. We throw quite a few parties, it seems. Maybe that's because we've got a collection of five cups in our trophy room, to say nothing of the Count's first, that I kind of like people to look at. Maybe it's because Jane is a swell girl that likes people, I don't know. Anyway, we're happy, she, I, and the little lady that was waiting upstairs, and that's a wonderful thing.